STORY AND ART BY

NORIYUKI KONISHI

ORIGINAL CONCEPT AND SUPERVISED BY LEVEL-5 INC.

YO-KAI WATCH™

Volume 12

BASHFUL YO-KAI MR. BLUE-SHY

VIZ Media Edition

Story and Art by Noriyuki Konishi

Original Concept and Supervised by LEVEL-5 Inc.

Translation/Tetsuichiro Miyaki
English Adaptation/Aubrey Sitterson
Lettering/John Hunt
Design/Shawn Carrico

YO-KAI WATCH Vol. 12
by Noriyuki KONISHI

Printed in the U.S.A.

Published by VIZ Media, LLC
P.O. Box 77010
San Francisco, CA 94107

10 9 8 7 6 5 4 3 2 1
First printing, September 2019

STORY AND ART BY
NORIYUKI KONISHI

ORIGINAL CONCEPT AND SUPERVISED BY LEVEL-5 INC.

CHARACTER INTRODUCTION

NATHAN ADAMS

AN ORDINARY ELEMENTARY SCHOOL STUDENT. WHISPER GAVE HIM THE YO-KAI WATCH, AND THEY HAVE SINCE BECOME FRIENDS.

WHISPER

A YO-KAI BUTLER FREED BY NATE, WHISPER HELPS HIM WITH HIS EXTENSIVE KNOWLEDGE OF OTHER YO-KAI.

JIBANYAN

A CAT WHO BECAME A YO-KAI WHEN HE PASSED AWAY. HE IS FRIENDLY, CAREFREE, AND THE FIRST YO-KAI THAT NATE BEFRIENDED.

BARNABY BERNSTEIN
NATE'S CLASSMATE.
NICKNAME: BEAR.
CAN BE MISCHIEVOUS.

EDWARD ARCHER
NATE'S CLASSMATE.
NICKNAME: EDDIE.
ALWAYS WEARS HEADPHONES.

USAPYON
A RABBIT-LIKE YO-KAI IN A SPACESUIT. HE CAME FROM THE COUNTRY OF BBQ.

HAILEY ANNE THOMAS
A FIFTH GRADER WHO IS A SELF-PROCLAIMED SUPERFAN OF ALIENS AND SAILOR CUTIES.

TOMNYAN
A MYSTERIOUS YO-KAI WHO ALSO COMES FROM THE COUNTRY OF BBQ. HE SEEMS TO HAVE AN ULTERIOR MOTIVE...

TABLE OF CONTENTS

CHAPTER 110: BASHFUL YO-KAI MR. BLUE-SHY

DING DINGDING DING DING
BYE! ♪
SEE YOU LATER! ♪
HEY KATIE! WANT TO WALK HOME TOGETHER? ♪
SURE! ♪
...
...
UMM... NATE...?
YEAH? W-W-WHAT'S UP?

WHY ARE YOU ALL THE WAY BACK THERE?

!!!

THIS ISN'T EXACTLY WALKING HOME "TOGETHER."

BASHFUL BASHFUL

YEAH...I KNOW... ♪

HEH HEH
IT'S JUST... TALKING TO YOU IS A LITTLE... EMBARAS-SING... ♪
HEH
HEH
REALLY? WE TALK TO EACH OTHER ALL THE TIME THOUGH!

SOMETIMES YOU GET TO TALKING TO YOURSELF AND YOUR WHOLE PERSONALITY CHANGES...IT LOOKS LIKE IT'S ONE OF THOSE DAYS, NATE. ♪

I'LL WALK THE REST OF THE WAY BY MYSELF. TALK TO YOU LATER! ♪

WHAAAAAAA

WHAT WAS I JUST DOING?!

AHHHHH!
THIS WAS MY BIG CHANCE TO TALK TO HER ALONE!

WHISPER! WHY DIDN'T YOU SAY ANY-THING?!
HUH? WHISPER?

WHERE DID HE GO...?

HUH?
SWIP

...
SHFF SHFF
WHY DO I FEEL LIKE SOME-ONE'S WATCHING ME?

FWAASH
COULD IT BE A YO-KAI?!

AH! THERE YOU ARE, WHISPER!
DO YOU SEE ANY YO-KAI?

WHAT?! YOU'RE NOT WHISPER! YOUR HEAD JUST LOOKS LIKE HIS!

WHO ARE YOU?!

AW SHUCKS... I'M NOBODY REALLY... ♪

BASHFUL BASHFUL

I NEVER THOUGHT I'D MEET A HUMAN WHO CAN SEE YO-KAI... ♪

WELL THEN, GOOD-BYE.

SWIP

EH...

CHAK
HOLD IT RIGHT THERE!
THUNGK
HUURGH!
GASP
YOU MUST BE THE REASON I WAS ACTING SO WEIRD!
HEH HEH HEH... ♪ OH IT WAS NOTHING. ♪
OOOOH...
STOP BLUSHING! I'M NOT COMPLIMENTING YOU!
BASHFUL BASHFUL
OH, REALLY? GUESS I GOT MIXED UP. ♪ HEHEHEH. ♪
IT'S STILL BLUSHING!
MY NAME IS, EH... EH...
MR BLUE-SHY. ANYONE INSPIRITED BY ME BECOMES UM... UM...
THEY BECOME SHY, RIGHT?
WHAT?

YOU'VE HEARD OF ME? REALLY?

BASHFUL

BASHFUL

BASHFUL YO-KAI
MR. BLUE-SHY

I'VE NEVER HEARD OF HIM, BUT IT WASN'T HARD TO FIGURE OUT!

WHERE'S WHISPER?! WHAT DID YOU DO WITH HIM?!
WHO'S WHISPER?
NATE! I'M OVER HERE...!
PEEEK
WHISPER!

I JUST...I FEEL TOO EMBAR-RASSED TO SHOW MYSELF...I DON'T KNOW WHY...
I'VE ALREADY FIGURED IT OUT. STOP WASTING TIME AND COME OUT HERE.
...
SHUPT

IF YOU SAY SO...
SHY SHY
FIDGET
FIDGET
...
WHAT?

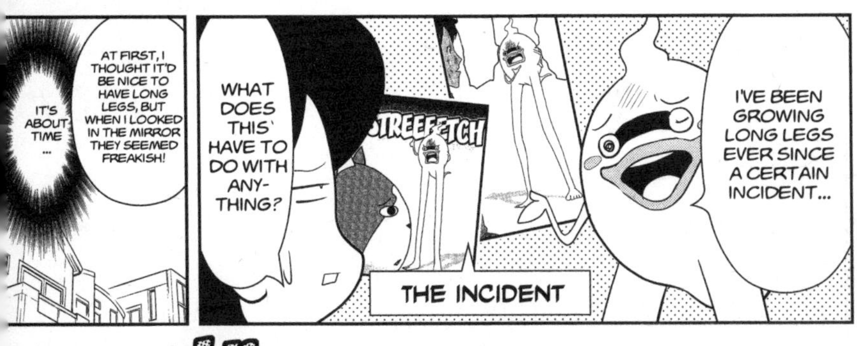

I'VE BEEN GROWING LONG LEGS EVER SINCE A CERTAIN INCIDENT...
THE INCIDENT
WHAT DOES THIS HAVE TO DO WITH ANYTHING?
AT FIRST, I THOUGHT IT'D BE NICE TO HAVE LONG LEGS, BUT WHEN I LOOKED IN THE MIRROR THEY SEEMED FREAKISH!
IT'S ABOUT TIME ...

THAT YOU REALIZED YOU LOOK ABSURD!!

HEY YOU! I'VE HAD MY EYE ON YOU!
!!!

HOW COULD YOU MAKE MY MASTER LOOK SO GROSS IN FRONT OF A GIRL?!
BAAAM
WHAT?
SHOCK
I LOOKED GROSS?!

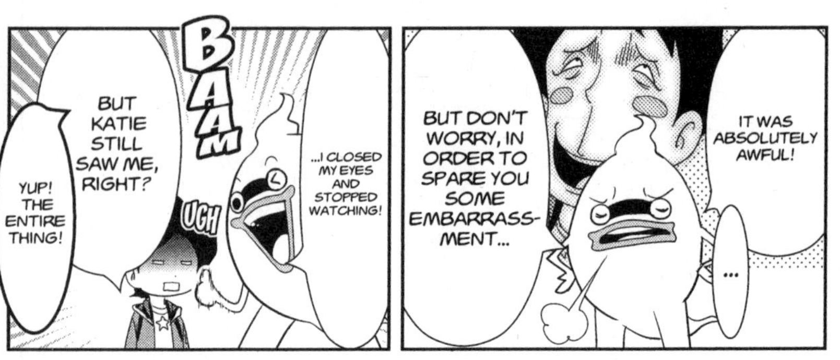

YOU'RE MY BUTLER, RIGHT?! WHY DIDN'T YOU STOP THIS YO-KAI FROM INSPIRITING ME?!
BASHFUL
BASHFUL
MY LEGS STARTED TO GROW AND...I JUST GOT SO EMBARRASSED...
FIDGET FIDGET
BUT YOUR MASTER WAS BEING EVEN MORE EMBARRASSED!

CALLING...
VNNNNN...
JIBANYAN!

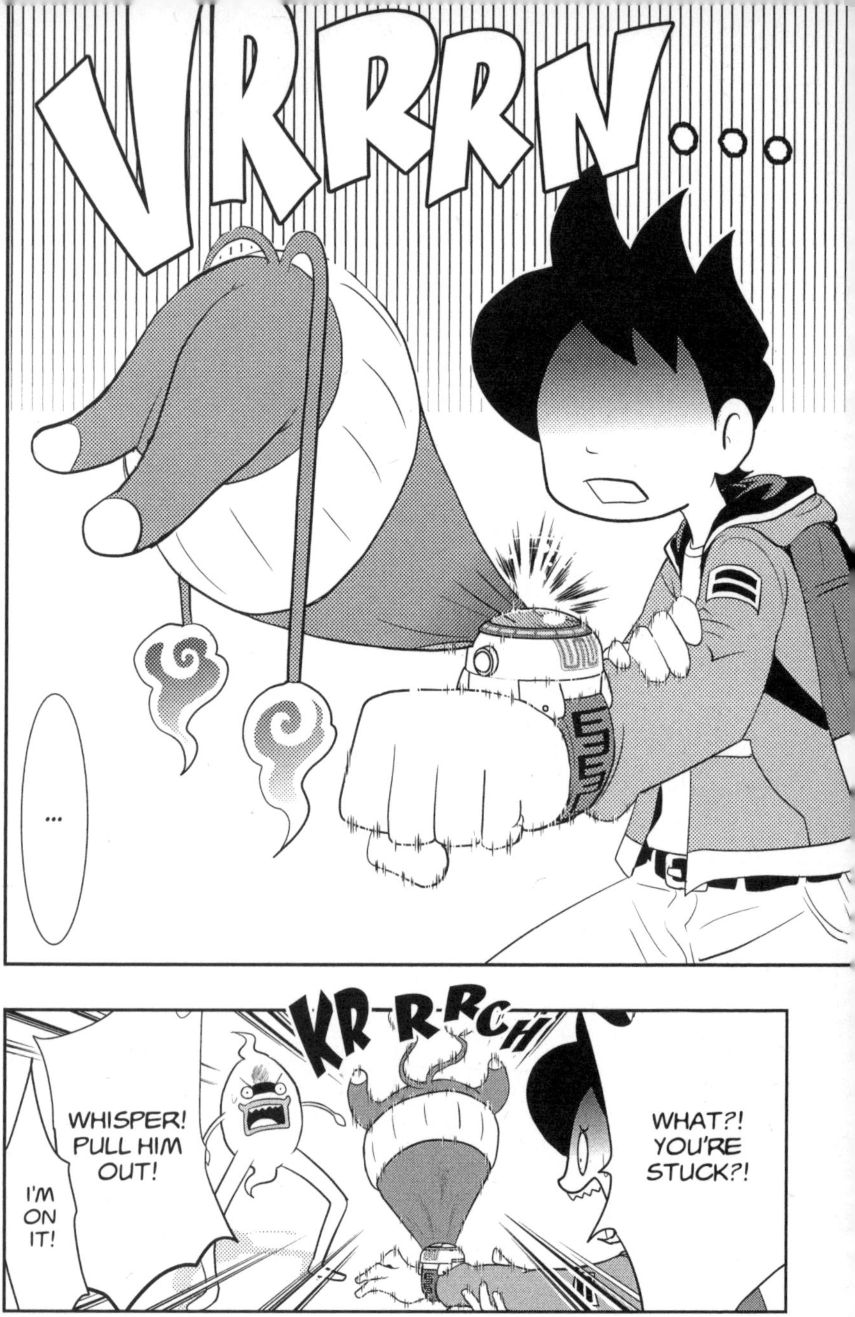

VRRRN...

...

CLOMP
STOP IT! DON'T TOUCH ME!
CLOMP
WE'RE TRYING TO HELP YOU OUT!
STREEEETCH
STREEEETCH
NOOOOOO! I DON'T WANT TO APPEAR IN THIS CHAPTER! I'M TOO EMBAR-RASSED!
COULD IT BE...
...HIS FAULT?!
SHUUPT
HE'S OUT!
MEEOOOW!
THAT WAS UNCALLED FOR!
HMM?

YOU'RE STILL SUFFERING FROM "THE INCIDENT" TOO?!

BAAAAM

DON'T LOOK AT ME!

THIS IS SO EMBARRASSING!!

SHOOM

I'LL NEVER FORGIVE YOU FOR THIS!

LOOK AT MY HEAD!

THAT'S WHY YOU'RE SO ANGRY...?

I WON'T FORGIVE ANYONE WHO GIVES NATE TROUBLE!

GRRRRRRRR!

!!!

THAT SNAPPED HIM OUT OF IT!

PAWS OF FURY!

FWOO
FWOO
FWOO
HEH HEH HEH... YOUR ATTACKS CAN'T HARM MY FLIMSY BODY.
I MIGHT BE BASHFUL. I MIGHT LOOK WEAK...
...BUT DON'T UNDER-ESTIMATE ME!
BASHFUL PUNCH!
!!

SHF
AHHH... I JUST CAN'T DO IT! I'M TOO EMBAR-RASSED TO GET INTO A FIGHT!
WHAT?!
THUNGKT
THIS DOESN'T MAKE ANY SENSE!
HEE-HEE... HOW EMBAR-RASSING...
I DIDN'T EVEN SEE WHAT HAPPENED!
NOW I KNOW THAT YOUR HEAD IS SOLID!
ONE MORE TIME...

PAWS OF FURY!
NO MATTER HOW MANY TIMES YOU TRY...YOU'LL NEVER HIT ME! ♪
YEAH? WELL, I'M NOT TRYING TO HIT YOU!
?!
WHAT?! I CAN'T MOVE!
GOTCHA! ♪
GLOMPT
HUUURGH!
YOU WERE AIMING FOR MY SCARF!
THAT'S A SCARF?!
I'LL JUST TAKE IT OFF...!
HUP!
TUG

TAKE THAT!
THU
NCKT

HNNGH

I GIVE UP...

I'VE NEVER HAD MUCH CONFI-DENCE IN MYSELF...
AND I'D BE SO EMBARRASSED IF I TRIED AND STILL FAILED...
SO I PROTECT MYSELF BY BEING BASHFUL...

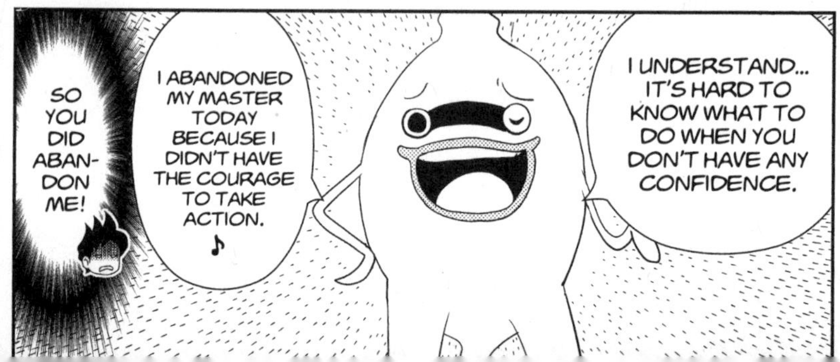

I UNDERSTAND... IT'S HARD TO KNOW WHAT TO DO WHEN YOU DON'T HAVE ANY CONFIDENCE.
I ABANDONED MY MASTER TODAY BECAUSE I DIDN'T HAVE THE COURAGE TO TAKE ACTION. ♪
SO YOU DID ABAN-DON ME!

MEOW. ♪ I WAS ABOUT TO ABANDON HIM TOO.
BUT I WAS ABLE TO MUSTER MY COURAGE BECAUSE I WANTED TO HELP MY FRIEND. ♪
JIBANYAN...
FRIENDS...

BASHFUL BASHFUL
PRK PRK
UHH, NATE... BY THE WAY... COULD YOU HURRY UP AND CALL **FURGUS**...?
THAT WAS HIS REAL MOTIVATION...

ANYWAY, LIKE YOU JUST HEARD,... EVERYONE KNOWS THAT FEELING. YOU SHOULD TRY TO HAVE A LITTLE MORE CONFIDENCE FROM NOW ON!
O-OKAY...
YOU GUYS ARE THE FIRST...
...TO EVEN ACTUALLY TALK WITH ME. ♪

I'M SO BASHFUL THAT I'VE NEVER REALLY HAD ANY FRIENDS...
I SEE...
WELL...

IF YOU WOULDN'T MIND YOUR FIRST FRIEND BEING A HUMAN...
...I'LL BE YOUR FRIEND!
!!!

REALLY? I THOUGHT YOU DIDN'T LIKE ME...!
THAT WAS BEFORE I GOT TO KNOW YOU! ♪

...

AND IT'S ONLY NATURAL TO TRY AND HELP SOMEONE STRUGGLING WITH SELF-CONFIDENCE!

I'VE NEVER MET SOMEONE WHO COULD SAY SOMETHING SO SINCERE WITHOUT BEING EMBAR-RASSED!
I SHOULD MUSTER MY COURAGE AND JUMP INTO HIS ARMS!

THANK YOU! ♪
SHUP

THUNK

URRGH!

OOOF!

I GOT A NEW YO-KAI MEDAL.
UMM... COULD YOU CALL FURGUS NOW?
DON'T... WORRY ABOUT IT...
TWITCH TWITCH...
I FORGOT ABOUT THE LUMP ON MY HEAD...HEE HEE. ♡
NATE ADAMS'S CURRENT NUMBER OF YO-KAI FRIENDS: 71

CHAPTER 111:
HUNGRY YO-KAI
HUNGRAMPS

HEY! HEY, HEY, HEY, HEY, HEY!
TUMP TUMP
TUMP TUMP TUMP TUMP
HEY! HEY, HEY, HEY, HEY, HEY!
HEY, HEY!
TUMP TUMP
TUMP TUMP
HEY, HEY!
HEY, HEY!
TUMP TUMP
TUMP TUMP
HEY, HEY!
HEY!!!
TUMP TUMP
TUMP TUMP
HEEEEEEEEY!

WHY HAVEN'T I BEEN IN THIS MANGA LATELY?!
I TOLD YOU THAT I WAS AN IMPOR-TANT CHARAC-TER, DIDN'T I?!
NOW, NOW ... ♪
MAYBE THEY'RE SAVING YOU FOR ONE OF THOSE ICONIC SCENES WHERE A CHARACTER RUSHES BACK IN TO SAVE THEIR FRIENDS! ♪
ARRRRRGH!!
BUT I'VE ALREADY DONE THAT...!
HMM ...
YO-KAI WATCH
8
YOU MEAN I'M ALREADY A STAR?
YOU'VE ALWAYS BEEN A STAR IN MY EYES!
YEAH!
AND SO, IN THIS CHAPTER ...
RMMMBLE

I, USAPYON, AM THE MAIN CHARACTER!
BUT...
NOW THAT I FINISHED MY ROCKET... THERE'S NOTHING LEFT FOR ME TO DO.
SNIFF
WHAT SHOULD I DO NOW...?
YOU SHOULD GO BACK TO BBQ.
THAT'S SO COLD AND CALLOUS!
WHAAAAA
YOU MONSTER! YOU MUST BE A HEARTLESS YO-KAI!
I'VE GROWN REALLY FOND OF THIS PLACE. AND OF YOU AND NATE TOO!
SO I'VE MADE A DECISION...
I BET THERE ARE OTHER YO-KAI THAT ARE IN TROUBLE, JUST LIKE I WAS!
SO I'M GOING TO TRACK THEM DOWN AND HELP THEM!
OOOH! IT'S YOUR WAY OF GIVING BACK! ♪
WE'LL SOLVE ANY PROBLEM!
INTRODUCING...

...THE HAPYON DETECTIVE AGENCY!!

THAT SOUNDS FUN! ♪

WAIT A MINUTE...! WAIT A MINUTE! IS THE "HA" PART SUPPOSE TO BE ME??!
WHAAA
HMMM HMMM
WELL THEN... LET'S SEE WHO'S IN TROUBLE!

YES! THERE'S A POOR ELEMENTARY SCHOOL GIRL WHO IS ABOUT TO GET FORCED INTO CHILD LABOR! SOMEONE HELP ME!

RABBLE RABBLE
WHAT'S THIS? THAT CONVENIENCE STORE HAS SUCH A LONG LINE!
LISTEN TO ME!

OH? THAT'S ...
!!

EVERYMART
YO-KAI WATCH VOLS. 1-12 NOW AVAILABLE!
HELP WANTED!
THERE'S A CONFUSED OLD MAN STANDING NEARBY!
BUT PEOPLE CUT IN LINE AND AREN'T LETTING HIM GET INSIDE!
THAT'S THE OLD MAN WHO HELPED US WHEN WE WERE LOOKING FOR DOCTOR HUGHLY!
YES?
!!!
OH! YOU'RE RIGHT!
WE HAVE TO REPAY OUR DEBT TO HIM!
HANG ON, OLD MAN! I'M ON MY WAY!
GWOOO
YOU'RE TAKING A ROCKET?! HE'S JUST DOWN THE BLOCK!
THE MAIN CHARACTER SHOULD ALWAYS MAKE A BIG ENTRANCE!
HUH?
!
HEY... WHAT?!
KLIK
KLIK

I'M ALL OUT OF BATTERIES! I CAN'T CONTROL THE ROCKET!
I CAN'T STOP! HELP MEEEEE!
BLINK
BLINK
GET OUT OF THE WAY, OLD MAN! QUICKLY!
?
I THOUGHT YOU WERE GOING TO HELP HIM...
FOR GOD'S SAKE! NOWAY, PLEASE!
DON'T STOP THAT ROCKET!
NOOOO WAAAY!
WOW! WHEN DID YOU BEFRIEND NOWAY?!
PLEASE DON'T STOP ME!
BAAM
NOOO WAAAY!
HE REFUSES TO DO FAVORS FOR YOU, SO HE'LL HELP YOU IF YOU ASK HIM TO DO THE OPPOSITE.

Nooo waaay...
You can do it
HUFF HUFF
CLOMPT CLOMPT
HE'S TOO FAR AWAY! THERE'S NO WAY HE CAN HELP ME!
AGGGH! THE OLD MAN'S JUST STANDING THERE!
WHAT? WHAT DID YOU SAY?
I HAVE NO CHOICE...
SELF-DESTRUCT!
HUUUH?
WHAT?!
I DON'T WANT TO HURT ANYONE!
PLIPT

NOOOO! WITHOUT ANY BATTERIES, I CAN'T EVEN SELF-DISTRUCT!
VWOOOSH
YOU IDIOT!
NO! PLEASE! OUT OF MY WAY!
NOOOO WAAAAY!
THOOM
NO-WAY!
WHERE DID YOU COME FROM?
PHEEE-EEW ...

THAT WAS CLOSE.
NATE!
NATE MUST HAVE SUMMONED HIM! ♪
WERE YOU WAITING IN THAT LINE TOO?
VNNNNNN
NOWAY, COULD YOU PUT ME DOWN SLOWLY—
THANKS A LOT...
WOOSH
NOOO WAAAAY!
OH NOO-OOO!
HE DOES THE OPPOSITE OF WHAT YOU TELL HIM.
OH NO...
DOOOM
AIYEEE!
...

HNNNGH
AND YOU THINK YOU'RE THE MAIN CHARAC-TER?
SIZZLE SIZZLE
NOWAY, DON'T LEAVE!
NOOO WAAAY ...
Thanks!
NATE!
WHAT ARE YOU DOING HERE?
I SUDDENLY GOT REALLY HUNGRY. BUT THERE WAS A HUGE LINE AT THE CONVENIENCE STORE...
...I DIDN'T REALIZE IT WAS BECAUSE OF A YO-KAI!
I WAS TOO HUNGRY TO EVEN THINK ABOUT IT!
THIS IS HUNGRY YO-KAI HUNGRAMPS.
YOUNG BOY AND GIRL, THANK YOU FOR HELPING ME!
AS A TOKEN OF THANKS...
SHF SHF
?
HUNGRY YO-KAI
HUNGRAMPS
PLEASE ACCEPT THIS!
OOH, A YO-KAI MEDAL!
LUCKY ME! ♪

WAIT... IT'S MONEY...?
GO TREAT YOURSELF TO SOMETHING NICE!
HE'S LIKE A REAL GRANDFATHER...
I... THANK YOU...
GRRUMBLE
GRRUMBLE
USE IT TO BUY YOURSELF A SNACK...
GRRUMBLE
GRRUMBLE
BUT YOU'RE SO HUNGRY! PLEASE USE IT TO GET YOURSELF SOMETHING TO EAT!
IT'S OKAY! I LIKE BEING HUNGRY IN FRONT OF THIS STORE.
?

EVERYMART

MY GRANDDAUGHTER AND I WOULD BUY LUNCH AND SNACKS HERE BACK WHEN I WAS STILL HUMAN...

MY **HUNGER** BRINGS BACK THOSE SWEET MEMORIES...

GRUMBLE

GRRUMBLE

SO DON'T WORRY ABOUT ME! GO GET YOURSELF SOME-THING TO EAT.

GRRUUMMBLE

GRRUMBLE

WE CAN'T HELP BUT WORRY!

WELL, YO-KAI CAN'T STARVE...
...AND HE'S HELPING THE STORE DO GREAT BUSINESS, SO WHAT'S THE HARM?
I guess you're right!
Thank you!

MAYBE WE CAN EAT SOMETHING TOGETHER WHEN WE'RE ACTUALLY HUNGRY! ♪
...
Good idea!

LET'S GO HOME AND EAT IT TOGETHER, GRANDPA!

YOU'VE HELPED ME RECALL A NEW MEMORY!
?
PLEASE, IN EXCHANGE FOR WHAT YOU'VE GIVEN ME...
SHUFF
OOH. ♪ THIS TIME IT'S FOR REAL!

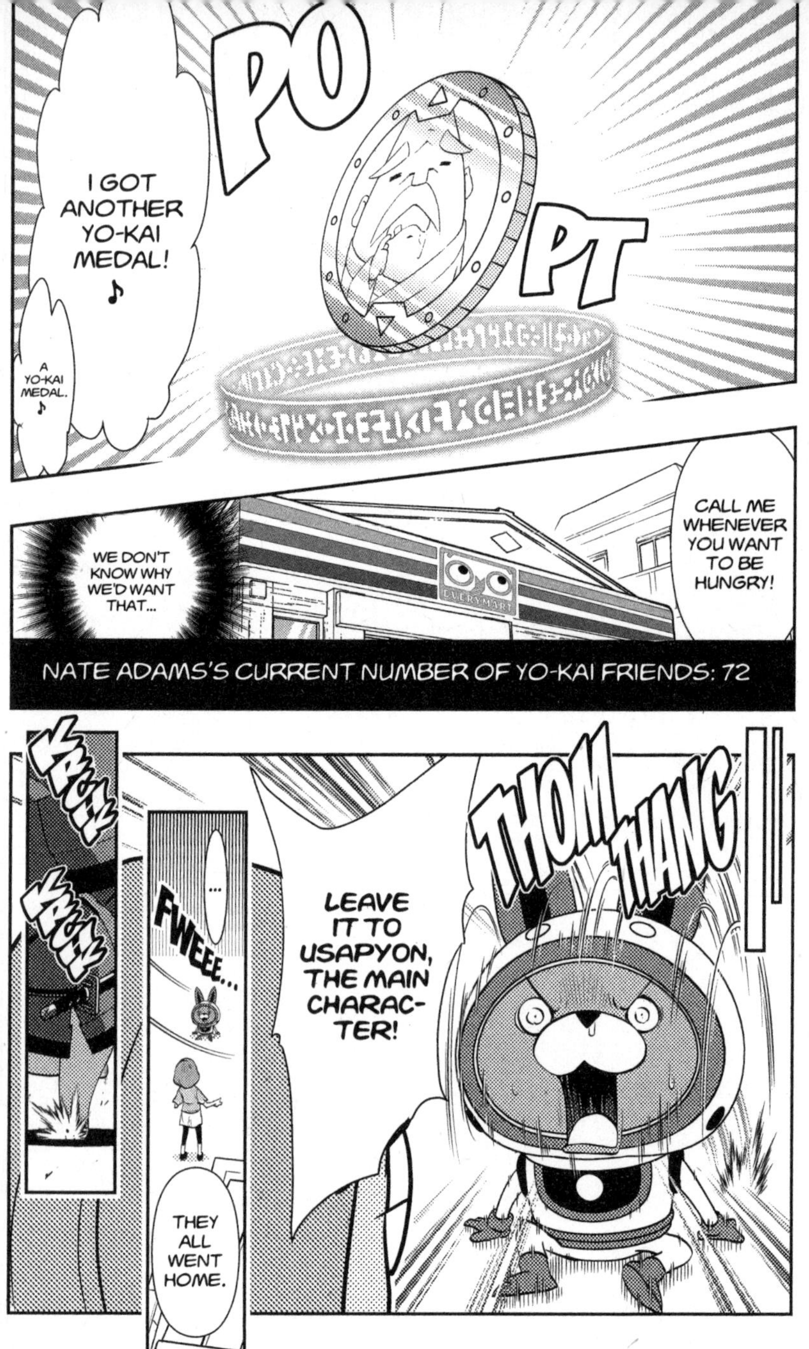
PO
PT
I GOT ANOTHER YO-KAI MEDAL! ♪
A YO-KAI MEDAL. ♪
CALL ME WHENEVER YOU WANT TO BE HUNGRY!
WE DON'T KNOW WHY WE'D WANT THAT...
EVERYMART
NATE ADAMS'S CURRENT NUMBER OF YO-KAI FRIENDS: 72
THOM
THANG
LEAVE IT TO USAPYON, THE MAIN CHARAC-TER!
...
FWEEE...
THEY ALL WENT HOME.
KRUK
KRUK

I'M THE MAIN CHARACTER, BUT I DIDN'T EVEN HELP!

WHAT A COLOSSAL FAILURE!

HE WAS SO EXCITED TO HELP...I FEEL BAD FOR HIM...

OH WELL! ♪ ARE THERE ANY OTHER YO-KAI IN NEED OF HELP? ♪

HE'S NOT DEPRESSED AT ALL!

KRCHK
HMM?

FWUMPT
HEY! WHAT'S WRONG?!
A YO-KAI?!
FWASH

GRRUMBLE
I'M SO... HUNGRY...
WHAT?! IT'S BECAUSE OF THAT OLD MAN!

SHUP...
URGH...
JUST HOLD ON!

WHAAA

AIYEEEE!! A MONSTER!

GRRUMBLE

DID YOU JUST CALL ME A MONSTER ?!
LOOK AT YOUR-SELF!

STAGGER

THAT'S SO...

SLASH

...RUDE OF YOU!

AIYEEE?!

WHAAAAAT?!

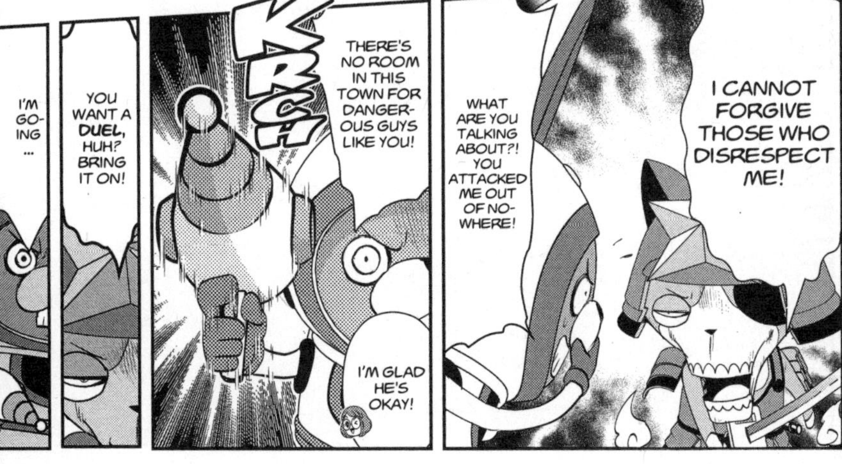

SLAASH

...TO BLAST YOU APART!

I THINK HE GOT TO YOU FIRST!

TWITCH

TWITCH

A TRUE **DUEL** CONTINUES UNTIL THE VERY END!

ARE YOU READY?

WAIT ...!

GRRRRR ...

CHAPTER 112: RICH YO-KAI FLASH T. CASH

FWUMP
...
I'M... SO...
...HUN... GRY...
HUH?
HNNGH
FWOO...
HE STARVED!
DUEL COMPLETE!
FWAAA
PHEEW
I FEEL BAD, BUT AT LEAST YOU'RE OKAY, USAPYON...
YOU TOO?!

SHE HEALS WOUNDS BY LICKING THEM.
SLUUSH SLUUSH
LICK LICK LICK
LICKETY-LICK. ♪
TONGUS!
TONGUS
!
Here!
AND THIS IS FOR YOU...
A RICE BALL!
!!!
THANK YOU SO MUCH!
MUNCH MUNCH CHOMP CHOMP MUNCH MUNCH
HUN-GRAMPS' MONEY CAME IN HANDY!
THAT WAS DELICIOUS!
EVERYMART
I FEEL GREAT!
WOW..., SO THAT'S HOW YOU ACTUALLY LOOK! ♪
SAMURAI YO-KAI
LAST NYANMURAI
GRRR-RRR! HOW DARE YOU!
!
THUNCK
I'VE HAD JUST ABOUT ENOUGH!
CALM DOWN, USA-PYON!
...

I'M THE MAIN CHARACTER HERE! HOW DARE YOU TAKE MY SPOT ON THE COVER OF THE VOLUME!
THIS IS UNACCEPTABLE!
THAT'S WHY YOU'RE MAD?! HE JUST CUT YOU IN HALF!
THANK YOU VERY MUCH. I OWE YOU A DEBT OF GRATITUDE FOR THE RICE BALL.
THEN PLEASE... FORGIVE USAPYON!
HE'S NOT EVEN LISTENING TO ME!
FOR THE GIRLS' SAKE, I SHALL FORGIVE YOU JUST THIS ONCE. BUT DON'T LET ME CATCH YOU BEING DISRESPECTFUL AGAIN!

ALL RIGHT! IT'S TIME TO OFFICIALLY OPEN THE HAPYON DETECTIVE AGENCY!
I'M GONNA DO IT!
HE'S NOT EVEN LISTENING!

THAT'S IT! I'M GOING TO SLICE HIM APART AGAIN!
KRRCHK
No! Please!
BUT FIRST THINGS FIRST...
I NEED TO REPAIR MY ROCKET SO I CAN MAKE A GRAND ENTRANCE!
DON'T FORGET BATTERIES FOR YOUR CONTROLLER!

WOW...IT'S REALLY BUSTED UP. I DON'T HAVE ENOUGH MONEY...
AW, MAN...
FWOO FWOO
HUH?
LOOK! MONEY'S FALLING FROM THE SKY!
WOW! AMAZING!
IF YOU THINK ABOUT IT, IT'S CLEAR WHAT'S HAPPENING.
YES, I SEE!
UH-HUH!

KRRCH KRRCH
IT'S MAGIC!
YEE-HAW!
SLAP
NO! IT'S A YO-KAI!
KRRCH KRRCH
HE'S OB-SESSED WITH WEALTH...
HMM.
FAAASH
MWA HA HA. ♪
MWA HA HA. ♪
RICH MAN! MAKE IT RAIN! FLASH T. CASH! ♪
FWOOSH FWOOSH
WADS OF MONEY! TONS OF MONEY! FLASH T. CASH! ♪
THERE HE IS! BUT WHAT A WEIRD SONG...
SOOOO MUCH MONEY! ♪ I'VE GOT MONEY TO BURN! ♪ MADE IT RAIN MONEY IN BBQ NOW I'M DOING IT AGAAAAAAAIN! ♪ JUST PICK IT UP! ♪ GO AHEAD AND TAKE IT! ♪
THEN...

MWA HAHA MWA HAHA
...REVERE ME! WORSHIP ME! GROVEL AT MY FEEEEEEEET! ♪
FWOOSH
THIS IS LUDICROUS!
FWOOSH
HE'S RIGHT! DO YOU REALLY THINK YOU CAN JUST BUY PEOPLE'S AFFECTION?!
BOO! BOO!
THAT'S TERRIBLE! IT'S GROSS! AND CHEAP!
WHY ARE YOU HIDING BEHIND ME...?
HA HA HA!
CHEAP...? DID YOU... JUST CALL ME... CHEAP?!
GRRR
LITTLE GIRL, LET ME TELL YOU ONE THING!
WHOA, HE'S REALLY ANGRY!
THERE IS ONE WORD... THAT I HATE... MORE THAN ANY OTHER WORD...
I THINK I CAN GUESS WHAT IT IS...
RRMBBLE

...MISERLYYYYYYY!
AHHHH
IT'S NOT CHEAP? THEN WHY IS HE SO ANGRY?!
I AM NOT SOME CREEP WHO WANTS TO BUY POPULARITY WITH MONEY!
I JUST THROW MONEY AROUND TO SHOW EVERYONE HOW WONDERFUL I AM! THAT WAY EVERYONE KNOWS TO ADORE ME!
THAT'S STILL AWFUL. AND HE SURE TALKS A LOT...
WHEN PEOPLE CAN'T APPRE-CIATE THAT...
...IT'S JUST SOUR GRAPES! THEY'RE JEALOUS OF ME!
SO I JUST SPEND MORE MONEY! I USE IT TO CRUSH THEM! AND IF THEY STILL WON'T BOW DOWN TO ME, I WIPE THEM OUT OF EXISTENCE!
"MONEY ISN'T EVERY-THING."
THAT'S JUST A LOUSY EXCUSE FROM PEOPLE WHO DON'T HAVE...

...MON-AIEE-EEE!
AAASH
ARRRRRRRGH!
D-D-DIDN'T MEAN IT?!
I'M SORRY...I DIDN'T MEAN IT. I JUST... COULDN'T HELP MYSELF.
AH!
ONLY COWARDS BASE THEIR SELF-WORTH ON MONEY!
LET THIS BE A LESSON TO YOU!
TWITCH TWITCH
GREAT JOB!
THAT WAS AWE-SOME!
HUH?!

I'M SO SORRY!
OH NOOOO! I'M THE MAIN CHARACTER BUT I WAS TEMPTED BY ALL THIS MONEY! I TOTALLY FORGOT TO HELP OUT!
DON'T WORRY. ANYONE BLINDED BY GREED SO EASILY PROBABLY WASN'T THE MAIN CHARACTER TO BEGIN WITH.
AW, DON'T LET IT GET TO YOU! EVERYONE MAKES A MISTAKE NOW AND AGAIN! ♪
YOU'RE STILL A GOOD GUY!
HE'S GIVING HIMSELF A PEP TALK?!
LAST NYANMURAI WOULD BE A MUCH BETTER MAIN CHARACTER THAN ME ANYWAY.
I KNEW IT...
I BELIEVE YOU'RE RIGHT.
WAIT IS HE TALKING DOWN ON HIMSELF NOW?
ENOUGH! WE'LL DECIDE WHO'S THE MAIN CHARACTER ONCE AND FOR ALL!
NOT AGAIN ...
VERY WELL! THIS TIME WE'LL FIGHT TO THE END!
ZUFF

CHAPTER 113: SNAP DECISION YO-KAI DECIDEVIBLE

THIS LOOKS REALLY SERIOUS, RIGHT? BUT IT'LL FIZZLE OUT QUICKLY.
IT'S SO OBVIOUS.

KA KA
SHA SHA
HE CUT THE LASER BEAM IN TWO!
CHKT...
CHKT...
...

CHOOM CHOOM CHOOM CHOOM
KRA-
DOOM
HEY... THIS IS GETTING REALLY INTENSE!

SHHHAAAA

NOT BAD... I DIDN'T REALIZE YOU WERE THIS GOOD...

RIGHT BACK AT YOU.

COULD... COULD THIS BE...

B-BMP B-BMP
...A BUDDING FRIENDSHIP?! BIRTHED OUT OF A NEWFOUND RESPECT FOR THEIR RIVAL?!
AND AFTER THIS THEY BECOME BLOOD-BROTHERS!! WHAT AN EXCITING SCENE!! OOOH!!

I WILL NEVER RELINQUISH MY TITLE AS MAIN CHARACTER OF THIS MANGA.

OH NO...!

I'M NOT INTERESTED IN BEING THE MAIN CHARACTER...

...BUT I REFUSE TO BACK DOWN!

OH NO...?

HAILEY ANNE!

YES, SIR!

WOOOSH

AS AN OUTSIDE OBSERVER...

...WHICH OF US IS BEST FIT TO BE THE MAIN CHARACTER?!

WHAT?! HOW CAN I CHOOSE?!

WELL...

STRENGTH ISN'T EVERYTHING... A MAIN CHARACTER ALSO NEEDS TO BE LIKABLE...

...MAKE THE DECISION FOR YOU...
VSSH
...IN THE BLINK OF AN EYE!
!!!
!!!
HMM... WHICH ONE...
...
SHE CAN'T SEE HIM WITHOUT THE WATCH!
HE DID HIS BIG POSE AND SHE'S GOING TO MISS IT!
WHAT?! A YO-KAI ?!
FWASH
...
WHOA! WHICH YO-KAI IS THIS?!
AND WHAT'S WITH THAT POSE ?!
WHAT'S HE GOING TO DO? WILL HE REPEAT HIMSELF?
THIS WILL BE INTER-ESTING...

NOW I MUST DECIDE ON WHETHER TO INTRODUCE MYSELF AGAIN OR NOT!
AND MY DECISION IS...I WILL!
HE SURE IS PERSISTENT, HUH?
THAT'S ONE WORD FOR IT...
BWAHAHAHA!
I AM THE INSTAN-TANEOUS, SNAP DECISION YO-KAI...
DECIDE-VIBLE!
SNAP DECISION YO-KAI
DECIDEVIBLE
...
DON'T WORRY! I'M USED TO PEOPLE BEING STUNNED BY MY PRESENCE!
MAYBE HE SHOULD WORRY SOME...
YOU'RE STUMPED TRYING TO DE-CIDE WHO SHOULD BE THE MAIN CHARAC-TER, RIGHT?!
I'LL MAKE THE DECISION FOR YOU! ♪
AND THE MAIN CHARACTER SHOULD BE...
Drumroll please!
BRRRRRLLLLLLL...

ME !!
Just kidd--
THAT'S ENOUGH.

YAAAAAOOOOW!
HE WAS IRRITATING ME AND FOR SOME REASON ...
...I IMMEDIATELY DECIDED TO ATTACK HIM.
URRGH ...
NICE WORK.
YUP.
BWA HA HA!
EXACTLY! DO YOU SEE?! YOUR SNAP DECISION IS ONLY FURTHER PROOF OF MY INCREDIBLE POWER!
AND NOW IT'S TIME TO SAY FAREWELL!
WHAT? THAT'S IT? AREN'T YOU GOING TO KEEP FIGHTING?!
I'D LOVE TO STAY, HOWEVER...
...I'VE ALREADY MADE UP MY MIND TO LEAVE...
?

...AND BEGONE! ♪
THE SWORD ATTACK GOT HIM.
WE'LL FIGHT HIM SOME OTHER TIME.
YEAH...
...

LENGTH (CONTINUED FROM PAGE 29)

HOW DO YOU LIKE IT?
SO FURRY... SO HAIRY...
I HATE IT!
THE LENGTH IS ALL WRONG! I LOOK RIDICU-LOUS!
HAIR GROWING YO-KAI
FURGUS

THE LENGTH ...?
HMMM

IT'S GOING TO LOOK PRETTY WEIRD IF I MAKE IT LONGER!
THINK ABOUT IT!
I'M TALKING ABOUT MAKING IT SHORTER!

CHAPTER 114:
TAKE A BREAK YO-KAI
RE-Q-PERATE

I'M NATE ADAMS.
AN ORDINARY ELEMENTARY SCHOOL STUDENT.
I'M NOT SUPER SMART BUT I'M NOT DUMB EITHER. I'M JUST ORDINARY.
I'M NOT GOOD AT SPORTS OR BAD AT THEM. I'M JUST ORDINARY.
I'M NOT EXCEPTION-ALLY POPULAR WITH THE GIRLS AT SCHOOL.
BUT IF THERE'S ONE THING...
I'M HOME.
...THAT'S NOT ORDINARY ABOUT ME...
IT'S WHAT I'M WEARING...
KRCHK
...ON MY LEFT ARM.
HEY! LET'S GO OUT AND LOOK FOR MORE YO-KAI! ♪
TOSS

FNUMPT

...

WHAT IS THIS, NATE?! SOME KIND OF OLD-TIMEY SITCOM GAG? COME HOME AND IMMEDIATELY TRIP?

N-NO, I... JUST SUDDENLY FELT...SO TIRED...

LET ME REST A MINUTE ...

WHAT ?!

ALL YOU DID WAS GO TO SCHOOL AND COME BACK HOME--NOTHING SPECIAL, TOTALLY ORDINARY--AND YOU'RE THIS TIRED?!

COULD IT BE...?!

FWAASH

I KNOW! IT MUST BE A YO-KAI!

NO! YOU'VE BECOME EXCEPTIONALLY WEAK, NATE!
AND THIS IS WHISPER.
THAT'S AMAZING!
WHAT IS?
A YO-KAI WHO THINKS HE'S MY BUTLER FOR SOME REASON.

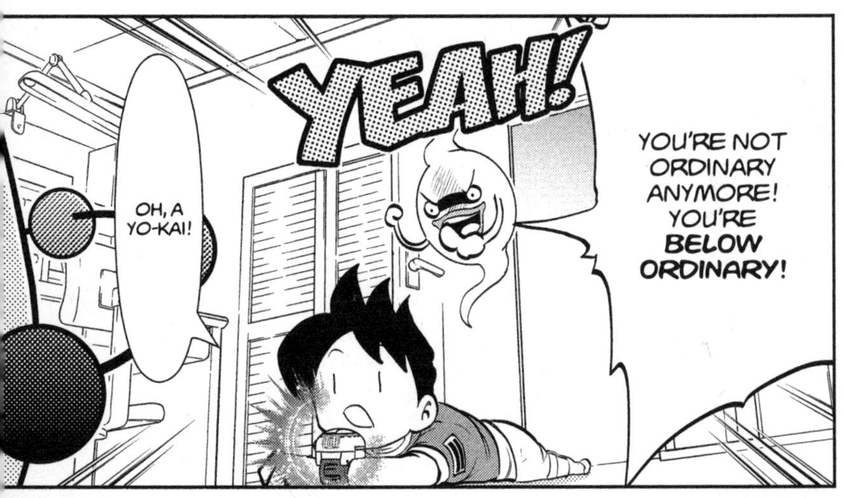

YOU'RE NOT ORDINARY ANYMORE! YOU'RE **BELOW ORDINARY**!
YEAH!
OH, A YO-KAI!

WELL?
AGH!
TWITCH
I'M AWAKE! I'M AWAKE!
HAS HE BEEN ASLEEP?

THAT MEANS ...

A YO-KAI THAT FORCES TIRED PEOPLE TO GET SOME REST!

THIS IS **RE-Q-PERATE!**

I FEEL SO BAD FOR YOU!

...THAT YOU'RE STILL TOTALLY ORDINARY, NATE!

HE'S SO AN-NOY-ING ...

NO! A YO-KAI BEING BEHIND THIS MEANS ...

I KNOW! HE'S THE REASON THAT I COLLAPSED AS SOON AS I CAME HOME!

?

HOW DISRE-SPECTFUL! MY MASTER NATE ADAMS WILL BEAT THE LIVING DAYLIGHTS OUT OF YOU!

SINCE WHEN DO I DO THAT?!

FWUUUMP
!!!

AGGRESSION AND IRRITABILITY ARE SIGNS THAT YOUR BODY IS TIRED!
SO I HELPED HIM GET SOME REST.

HE'LL BE ASLEEP FOR A WHILE.
NGH...
IMPOSSIBLE! HOW IS HE UP ALREADY?!

...

NNGH...

IT'S JUST A LUMP!

UGGGH
FATIGUE BUILDS UP INSIDE YOUR BODY EVEN WHEN YOU DON'T REALIZE IT.
YOU DON'T FEEL TIRED BUT YOU PASS OUT ON THE COUCH...
YOU STRUG-GLE TO GET UP IN THE MORNING...
I'M SURE IT'S HAPPENED TO YOU BEFORE!
IS IT ALL BECAUSE OF YOU?!
THA-AAT'S RIGHT.

YOU FORCE PEOPLE TO LIE DOWN AND SLEEP...YOU'RE KIND OF LIKE **CUTTA-NAH** AND **HORIZON-TAIL!**
THE YO-KAI THAT MAKES YOU LAZY? AND THE ONE THAT MAKES YOU THINK EVERYTHING IS BORING?

DON'T YOU DARE COMPARE ME TO THEM!
TAKE A BREAK YO-KAI
RE-Q-PERATE
THEY JUST MAKE PEOPLE LOUNGE AROUND IDLY!
!!!
I HELP PEOPLE REST SO THEY CAN REGAIN THEIR STRENGTH!
I'M IMPORTANT! I HELP PEOPLE LIVE THEIR LIVES TO THE FULLEST!
DON'T TREAT ME LIKE THOSE NO-GOOD SCOUNDRELS!
NO-GOOD SCOUNDRELS?! HOW COULD YOU SAY THAT?!
THEY'RE JUST TRYING TO LIVE THEIR LIVES TO THE FULLEST TOO!
HOW ABOUT YOU TELL THEM THAT TO THEIR FACES?

CALLING CUTTA-NAH AND HORIZON-TAIL!

UGH... WHAT IS IT? THIS IS ALREADY SUCH A DRAG.
HNNURRGH
YEAH...COULD WE TAKE MORE OF A BREAK BETWEEN SUMMONINGS? A HUNDRED YEARS OR SO?
COME ON, TELL HIM!
TELL HIM THAT YOU'RE NOT NO-GOOD SCOUN-DRELS!

I DON'T REALLY CARE EITHER WAY. THIS IS A REAL DRAG.
YEAH, I DON'T REALLY HAVE THE ENERGY TO GET UPSET ABOUT STUFF LIKE THAT.
Call me a scoundrel, whatever...
REALLY ...?
GOING ALL THE WAY HOME WOULD BE A DRAG, SO I'M GOING TO SLEEP HERE.
ME TOO.
OH, I'M... SORRY FOR SUMMON-ING YOU, I GUESS.
HAHA...I GUESS I WAS OVER-THINKING THINGS...!
...
!!!
...
WAIT...DID YOU JUST MAKE THEM GO TO SLEEP?!

PLIPT
AGH!
I'M AWAKE! I'M AWAKE!
HOW LONG HAVE YOU BEEN ASLEEP?!
SHFF
SHFF
DO YOU WANT TO MAKE PEOPLE REST OR DO YOU WANT TO TAKE A NAP? WHICH IS IT?!
...
TWITCH
AGH!!
YOU FELL BACK ASLEEP THAT QUICKLY?!
DEALING WITH YOU IS EXHAUST-ING!
JUST GET OUT OF HERE!
HEH HEH HEH, I'M... EXHAUST-ING?

AH—HA
EVERYONE SAYS THAT. BUT DON'T WORRY... ♪
...I CAN HELP YOU GET SOME REST! ♪
YOU'RE CREATING PROBLEMS JUST TO SOLVE THEM!
ALL RIGHT THEN...I'LL FORCE YOU TO LEAVE!
ROBO-NYAN NEVER GETS TIRED!
VOOSH
BUT HE DOES TEND TO RUN OUT OF BAT-TERIES EASILY...
KRRRKT
SO LET'S CALL SOMEONE ELSE! SHOW ME WHAT YOU CAN DO!
CALLING ...
... TOMNYAN!
MEEOOOW!

YOU NEED TO FIGHT A YO-KAI?
BUT WHY ME?
I THINK YOU'RE JUST THE YO-KAI TO BEAT HIM!
YOU THINK SO MUCH OF ME! WHAT AN HONOR! ♪
...
IF I HELP HIM NOW...
...I CAN CALL IN A FAVOR LATER TO HELP WITH MY TRUE PLANS!
CRYPTIC YO-KAI
TOMNYAN
VOOOSH
LET'S DO IT!
BE CAREFUL! THAT YO-KAI CAN MAKE YOU FALL ASLEEP!
QWEEEE
THE LIGHT! IT'S WHAT KNOCKED WHISPER OUT!

WOOOSH
NOT SO FAST!
FWUMP
WHY IS HE IN THE MIDDLE OF THE FLOOR?!
BUMPT
LOOKS LIKE I HAVE TO SUMMON ROBONYAN ANYWAY!
KRCH
...
...
AW MAN ...
Z Z Z
WHOOPS.

AHHH

...

HMM... YOU'RE NOT EVEN TRYING TO FINISH THEM OFF, ARE YOU?

WAIT... ARE YOU SLEEPING AGAIN?!

I DON'T SEE THEM AS MY ENEMIES. I JUST WANT TO HELP THEM GET SOME REST!

...

I SEE...I ASSUMED THAT WE WERE GOING TO HAVE TO FIGHT HIM...

...BUT HE DOESN'T MEAN ANY HARM.

YOU'VE ALREADY HELPED SO MANY YO-KAI... MORE THAN ANY OTHER HUMAN!

YOU SHOULD GET SOME REST EVERY NOW AND THEN!

THANKS... AND I'M SORRY.

YOU WERE GETTING IRRITATED EARLIER TOO...
....AND YOU KEPT FALLING ASLEEP! YOU MUST BE TIRED AS WELL!
SOUNDS LIKE YOU'RE THE ONE WHO NEEDS SOME REST! ♪
!!!

NOW I KNOW WHY HE HAS THE YO-KAI WATCH!
REST...NO HUMAN HAS EVER BEEN CONCERNED FOR ME BEFORE...

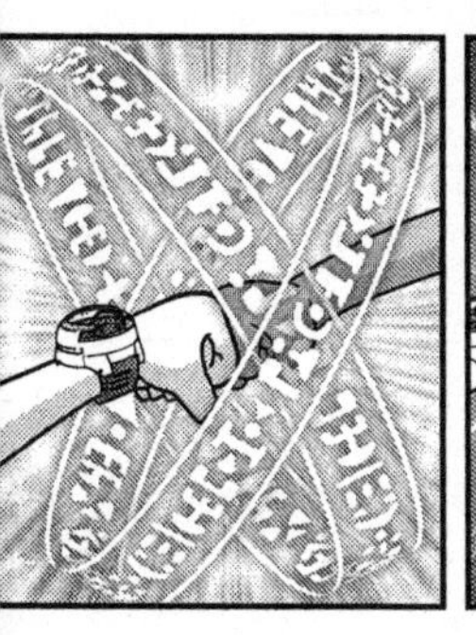

QWEEE...
QWEEE...
HUUUFF...
HUUUFF...
THERE'S NO ROOM FOR ME...
GRRRN
GRRRN
ZZZ...
TWITCH TWITCH

NATE ADAMS'S CURRENT NUMBER OF YO-KAI FRIENDS: 73

CHAPTER 115: KLUTZ YO-KAI CLODZILLA

MRRRAO-OWWW!
THUNCK!
SHUFF
WHOOPS.
ARRARRRRR
GH!
MY ARMS WERE TOO SHORT AND I ACCIDENTALLY HEAD-BUTTED HIM!
KLUTZ YO-KAI
CLODZILLA
FWOO
WHAT? THERE'S A STRANGE RING AROUND HIS BUTT!
NNNGH...
OH...
ARE YOU OKAY? I'M SO SORRY... I'M A KLUTZ YO-KAI AND ALWAYS MESS THINGS UP.
CLOMP CLOMP

HIS ESSENCE IS ESCAPING FROM HIS REAR!
SHOOOO
WHAAAA
MNGH MNGH
I'LL GRAB IT AND PUT IT BACK IN HIS BODY!
GRRN...
SHA
SHA
WHAT SHOULD I DOOO-OOO?!
SHOOOOO

KRAK!
TUNCK!
WHA?!
MRRRAAOOOW!

THE TELE-PHONE POLE!
KA-
UNNNGH
I MEAN... YOU'RE A YO-KAI...SO YOU'LL BE OKAY... RIGHT?
Heh heh heh...
HUNH?

SHOOOO
ANOTHER ONE!
How did his essence end?!
SHU NKT
I KNOW!
SH UP
I'LL MAKE HIM SWALLOW IT!

SHOOOOO
IT PASSED RIGHT THROUGH!
WHAAAA ARGH!
MEOW?!
Did the truck beat me again?!
SHUFF SHUFF SHUFF
I DON'T WANT TO BE GONE!
I'LL THROW YOUR BODY UP TO YOU!! GET IN THERE!
TEKT...
DO IT FAST!
HERE GOES!
THANK YOU!
SH

THAT'S TOO FAST!

AHHH ...!

I BARELY MANAGED IT.
PHEW...
I WAS ABOUT TO... YOU KNOW!
I'M SORRY ...
BOW
PEOPLE WHO ALWAYS MESS THINGS UP MIGHT BE UNDER THE EFFECT OF CLODZILLA!

CHAPTER 116:
UNINTENTIONAL YO-KAI
PUSH PUP
PLIP
I DID IT AGAIN! I WENT AND BOUGHT SOMETHING ELSE I DON'T NEED!
THE INTERNET MAKES IT TOO EASY THOUGH! I CAN BUY ANYTHING I WANT WITH THE CLICK OF A BUTTON! ♪
UNNNGH
TWITCH TWITCH
HRRRNGH
BEATEN BY A TRUCK... ONCE AGAIN ...
...SO I'LL GO...TEASE WHISPER... THAT'LL MAKE ME...FEEL BETTER...
STAGGER...
VMMMM

VNNN
NGKT
AIYEEEEE!
WHAAAA
HEY, CAT! WHY DON'T YOU WATCH WHERE YOU'RE WALKING?!
UNNNGH
WATCH WHERE I'M WALKING? YOU SHOULD WATCH WHERE YOU'RE DRIVING!
WHAT?
WATCH WHERE I'M DRIVING ...?
I WAS IN THE MIDDLE OF SHOPPING ON MY COMPUTER!
IT WAS TOTALLY OBVIOUS THAT I WASN'T WATCHING THE ROAD!
SO YOU SHOULD HAVE GOTTEN OUT OF THE WAY!
...

KRASHT!

VRRROOM

ARRRRRRGH!

UNINTENTIONAL YO-KAI

PUSH PUP

UNNGH!!

HEY! YOU SHOULD WATCH WHERE YOU'RE DRIVING!
VROOM
YOU JUST TOLD ME THE OPPOSITE ...
SHUT IT!
THIS IS YOUR FAULT TO BEGIN WITH!
ARRRRRGH!

WHERE... DID YOU EVEN... GET THAT...?!

I FOUND IT. I WASN'T PLANNING ON IT, BUT IT WAS JUST SO EASY!

Too easy...

YOU **JUST HAPPENED** TO BUY SUCH A THING ?!

I WAS WORRIED THAT IT WAS JUST GOING TO SIT AROUND TAKING UP SPACE FOREVER...

THANKS FOR GIVING ME AN EXCUSE TO USE IT! ♪

WHAAAT?! THERE WAS NO EXCUSE FOR THAT!

DO YOU MIND IF I TAKE THIS OPPORTUNITY ...

...TO USE THIS TOO?
WHAAAAAA?
A TANK?! WHAT?! OF COURSE I MIND!
KRRCH KRRCH
I JUST HAPPENED TO BUY THIS ONLINE AS WELL... ♪
NO! STOPPIT!
PLIP
FIRE!
THAT'S IT! I'LL PUNCH THE SHELL BACK AT YOU!
CHOOM CHOOM
CHOOM
CHOOM
PAWS OF FURY!

ZAP!
IT SHOOTS LASER BEAMS!
OH, IT FIRES SHELLS TOO!
BLAM
WHOA!
VOOOSH
KRA-DOOM
DON'T DODGE IT! IT'S DANGER-OUS!
WHAT?! OF COURSE IT'S DANGER-OUS!

THOOM

ARRRRRGH!

HRRNNGH
I SHOULD HAVE GOT THE TANK... WITH A ROOF ON IT...
IS THAT EVEN A THING?
MAYBE YOU SHOULD BUY SOME MEDICINE FIRST...
BE CAREFUL WHAT YOU BUY ON THE INTERNET!

CHAPTER 117:
ON THE EDGE YO-KAI
HUMTEA JUMTEA
THE TRUCK BEAT ME... AGAIN...
TWITCH TWITCH
TWITCH
VRRRROOM
AT LEAST I DIDN'T...
Yes, I know I'm already a Yo-kai.
VRRR
OOOM
WHO-EVER YOU ARE, PLEASE HELP ME!
HOLD ON! I'LL SAVE YOU!
JUST LEAVE IT TO ME!
VRROOOOM
FINISHED! DONEZO! NO WAY OUT OF A BAD SITUATION!
AGH! I SPOKE TOO SOON! IT'S GAME OVER FOR ME!

I'M GONNA DO IT! REALLY I AM!
TWITCH TWITCH
HUFF
HUFF
SHUDDER SHUDDER
Just hold on!
COME ON ALREADY! HURRY UP!
HUFF HUFF
I'M REALLY GOING TO DO IT! REALLY!
JUST DO IT!
HUFF HUFF
I'M REALLY, REALLY-- OH.
THUMP
ARRRRGH!
...
I...I DIDN'T SAVE HIM. BUT IF I HAD JUST RUSHED IN... WE BOTH WOULD HAVE BEEN HIT.
SO I MADE THE RIGHT CHOICE...
HMM?

WHY DID YOU EVEN BOTHER GETTING MY HOPES UP?!

NNNNNGH

OH NO! HE'S STILL ALIVE! AND ANGRY! HE'S GOING TO CLOBBER ME!

IT'S GAME OVER!

I HAVE NO OTHER OPTION...I HAVE TO DO IT...I HAVE TO APOLOGIZE SINCERELY!

I'M SORRY! ANYONE I INSPIRIT GETS CONFRONTED WITH A DIRE SITUATION!

SO THIS WAS ALL YOUR FAULT!

YES... I'M SO SORRY!

ON THE EDGE YO-KAI

HUMTEA JUMTEA

I WAS SO SCARED...I COULDN'T EVEN MOVE!

SHFF SHFF

FOR STARTERS, JUST COME DOWN HERE!

STOP LOOKING DOWN ON ME! IT'S RUDE!

OH NO! IT'S GAME OVER! I THOUGHT HE'D FORGIVE ME IF I WAS HONEST!
EEEEEK!
I'M NOT GOING DOWN THERE!
I KNOW HE'LL CLOBBER ME! BUT AS LONG AS I STAY AWAY, I'LL BE SAFE! I'M GOING HOME—!
HUH?
PLIP PLIP

TOO LATE! I CLIMBED UP!
ARRRRGH!
HRRRNG
CLIMB CLIMB
IT'S GAME OVER! HE'S GOING TO PUNCH ME! AND KICK ME! HE'LL KNOCK MY SPIRIT OUT OF MY BODY!
WHAT ON EARTH ARE YOU BABBLING ABOU--?!
SLLLLIPPT
!!!
MEOOOOOW!
FWOOOO
...
IS THIS YOUR FAULT TOO ?!
...
THIS... THIS TIME I'LL SAVE YOU!
BUNGEE JUUUUUMP!
VOOSH
!
BUNGEE JUMP! A TEST OF COURAGE IN WHICH YOU WRAP A CORD AROUND YOUR LEG AND JUMP FROM A HIGH PLACE.
FWOOO
HANG ON!
CLOMPT
THANKS!

THOOOM
WHOOPS...
THE ROPE WAS TOO LONG...
ARRRRRRRGH!
CLOUD! UP-UP-UP! QUICKLY!
TUG
TUG
TWITCH TWITCH
!!!
ARE YOU ALL RIGHT?!
THIS TIME I...I JUMPED DOWN TO HELP HIM! HE SHOULD FORGIVE ME... RIGHT?
NNNNGH...
IF YOU HADN'T INTER-FERED... I WOULD HAVE BEEN ABLE TO LAND PROP-ERLY!
RRMBBL
NOW HE'S MAD!
IT'S GAME OVER!

BUT THANKS FOR AT LEAST TRYING TO HELP!

ALL THE TROUBLE YOU'VE CAUSED ME...I FORGIVE YOU.

WHAT...?!

I MADE IT THROUGH... THIS HORRIBLE SITUATION...!

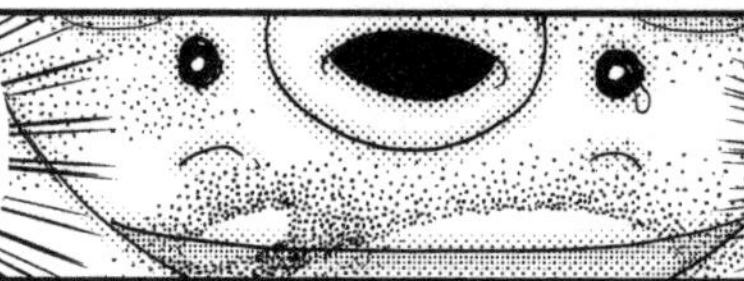

I THOUGHT IT WAS GAME OVER...BUT I MUSTERED ALL MY COURAGE! ♪

VRROOM
...
THUNGK
ARRRRGH!

SWWNNG
SWWNNG

URGH...
SNIFF SNIFF
ARE YOU OKAY?

YOU'RE SUCH A NUISANCE!
HUFF HUFF
THIS IS ALL BECAUSE I INSPIRITED YOU!
WHAT IS HE BLAMING ME FOR?!
I'M GONNA CLOBBER YOU!
VOOOOSH
ARE YOU KIDDING ME?! YOU'LL REGRET THIS!
SHUMP
YAAAAAAAAAAH!
WHOOOSH

WHOOPS ...
...
SPROOOING!
AHHHH!
P-TOWWWING
NNNNNGH...
ARRRGH!! CLOUD! COME DOWN! DOWN, I SAID! DOWN!
I'M GOING HOME.
ARRRRRRGH!
THU NGKT
VRROO

CHAPTER 118: BATH LOVER YO-KAI LIL BLUE BATHING HOOD

SHWAAA

WHAAAAAA?!

YOU'RE TAKING A BATH IN THE MIDDLE OF THE STREET?!

YEAH! YEAH! YEAH! YEAH!

IT'S MY LUCKY DAY! ♪ MAKE SOME ROOM! I'M COMING IN! ♪

WOOHOO!♪

WHAAAAAT?! USUALLY PEOPLE THINK I'M WEIRD FOR BATHING IN PUBLIC! THEY JUST STOP AND STARE!

AND NOT ONLY THAT... THEY ALSO THINK I'M WEIRD FOR WEARING A HOOD IN THE BATH! THEY WON'T EVEN LOOK AT ME!

RRRMM

BBLLEEE

IS THAT SO...?
AHHHHHHHHHH
WHAAA?!
HE'S ALREADY GOTTEN IN AND COMFORTABLE!

YOU'RE SUPPOSED TO RINSE YOURSELF BEFORE GETTING IN A PUBLIC BATH!

I KNOW... BUT I JUST COULDN'T HELP MYSELF!

SCRUB SCRUB
IT FEELS SOOOOOO GOOD. ♪
SO YOU NOTICED!

TEMPERATURE, WATER PURITY, WATER HARDNESS, THE AMOUNT OF WATER... EVERYTHING ABOUT THIS BATH IS PERFECT. ♪
I AM A YO-KAI THAT SOOTHES PEOPLE BY GIVING THEM THE PERFECT BATHING EXPERIENCE!

I LOVE BATHS SO MUCH THAT THIS TUB IS ACTUALLY PART OF ME! ♪
BATH LOVER YO-KAI
LIL BLUE BATHING HOOD
THE TUB IS PART OF YOU?!
YOU MUST BE EXAGGERATING!
WHAT?! ARE YOU SERIOUS?!

SHUPT
NOT A BIT! LOOK...

MY LEGS ARE DOWN HERE... AND UP THERE!
I EVOLVED AN EXTRA PAIR! ♪
HAHA!
...
AGGGGH! WHEN I STOOD UP, ALL THE WATER POURED OUT!
SPLOOOOO!
...

SHWAAA

I HAVE TO FILL IT BACK UP!

WAIT...IF YOU AND THE TUB ARE FUSED TOGETHER... WHERE DOES THE WATER COME FROM?

OH, THIS?

IT'S ALL THE WATER AND OTHER DRINKS THAT I'VE HAD IN THE PAST DAY OR SO! ♪

HAHAHA ♪

YOU MEAN YOU'RE TAKING A BATH IN YOUR **PEE?!**

WHAAAAAA!!

NO! NO
NO NO NO!
IT'S NOT!
IT'S NOT
PEE! IT'S
NOT!
SWIPT
SHWAAAA
AHHH!
IT'S
HOT!
IT'S HOT,
DIRTY
PEE!
IT IS
NOT!
HEH HEH HEH. ♪
WHEN I GET
MAD, THE
WATER
TEMPERATURE
RISES. ♪
SIZZLE SIZZLE
BUT
THANKS
TO
YOU...
?

AHHHHHH
NOW THE TUB IS NICE AND STEAMY! ♪
Climb on in! ♪
I'M NOT GETTING IN YOUR **HOT PEE BATH!**
SHWAA
AGGGGGH!
IT'S NOT PEE!
PLIP-PLIP
OH...
HMMMM
AWWW
I'M ALL OUT OF WATER...
OF COURSE YOU ARE! YOU CAN'T JUST KEEP PEEING FOREVER!
I AL-READY TOLD YOU...
THE STOPPER ...?
POPT

IT'S NOT PEE! DRAINAGE ATTACK!
FWOOOOOSH!
AGGGGH, IT'S HOT! AND IT'S COMING OUT OF HER BUTT! GROSS!
NO, IT'S NOT!
HUFF HUFF
SO RUDE!
TMP TMP
MY SWEAT GOT WASHED AWAY...
NNNGH
...BUT NOW I NEED ANOTHER BATH TO WASH AWAY THE PEE!

CHAPTER 119: UNPREDICTABLE YO-KAI UNBELIEVABOY!

HAHAHA
YOU'RE SO WEIRD...IT'S UNBELIEV-ABLE!
WALKING AROUND NAKED IN THE COLD?! YOU'RE THE ONE WHO'S WEIRD!
TA-DAAH
I'M UNBELIEV-ABOY!!!
A YO-KAI THAT LOVES SURPRISING PEOPLE BY DOING THE UNEX-PECTED!
UNPREDICTABLE YO-KAI
UNBELIEVABOY!
He usually wears a diaper.
UNBELIEVABLE!
BUCK NAKED IN THE MIDDLE OF WINTER! ARE YOU SURPRISED? PRETTY UNBELIEVABLE, HUH?
YOU'RE GOING TO CATCH A COLD...
OH, I'LL BE FINE. ♪
BUT...

SHIVER SHIVER SHUDDER SHUDDER

...FOR SOME REASON, I SUDDENLY GOT A CHILL, MY THROAT HURTS AND I CAN'T STOP SHIVERING...

Am I imagining this?

THAT'S TOTALLY A COLD.

OH COME ON! IT CAN'T BE THAT! IMPOSSIBLE!
KOFF KOFF
BEEP
ICE
YOU'RE DOING EXACTLY WHAT PEOPLE WITH COLDS DO!
REALLY?! THAT'S UNBELIEVABLE!

ANYWAY, LET'S CHANGE THE SUBJECT...
I CAN FLY, YOU KNOW!
WHAT? THAT CAME OUT OF NOWHERE...
ARE YOU SURPRISED? PRETTY UNBELIEVABLE, HUH?
FWOOM
AH-HA!
YOUR CAPE! THAT MUST BE HOW YOU FLY!
HA HA HA.

THIS? THIS IS TO PROTECT ME FROM THE COLD!

I can't survive without it.

SHIDDER SHIDDER

SHIDDER

SO HE IS COLD AFTER ALL!

TREMBLE TREMBLE

PUT SOMETHING ELSE ON!

WELL... HOW DO YOU FLY THEN?

EASY! ♪

I HOLD MY BREATH...

HUPT

SQUAT DOWN...

SHF

CLENCH MY STOMACH MUSCLES...

GRRN...

...

YAH!
POOOOOF
HE FARTS ?!
UGGGH
PRETTY AMAZING, RIGHT? ♪
P-P-POOF
ARE YOU SURPRISED? TOTALLY UNBELIEVABLE, ISN'T IT?!
...
MOOF
MOOF
MOOF
POOF POOF POOF
I CAN FLY AS SLOW OR FAST AS I WANT JUST BY ADJUSTING MY FARTS. ♪
UNBELIEVABLE, RIGHT?
IT'S... PRETTY IMPRES-SIVE ...
...BUT NOTHING TO BE PROUD OF. OR BRAG ABOUT. OR SHOW TO PEOPLE.
OH NO ...

IF I CAN'T FART...I FALL!
POOT
FWOOOO
WHAAAAT?!
MEOW?! IT'S A TRUCK!
LOOK OUT!

ULPT...

BURPS MAKE YOU FLY TOO?!

BUURRP

WHY MEEEEEE?!

THUN

GKT

UNBE-LIEV-ABLE...!

CHAPTER 120:
HERBIVORE YO-KAI
HERBIBOY
I'VE BEEN FIGHTING TRUCKS FOR SO LONG... BUT NOW IT'S TIME TO STOP.
INSTEAD, I THINK I'LL THANK THE CARS FOR GIVING ME SO MUCH ENTERTAIN-MENT.
AH, THERE IT IS NOW.
VRROOM...
MR. TRUCK, THANK YOU FOR--
THUNGK
ARRRRRGH!
HNNGH
TWITCH
TWITCH...
I DON'T... GET IT...

I KNOW...!
I DON'T FEEL LIKE FIGHTING OR DOING ANYTHING!
THERE MUST BE A YO-KAI AROUND!
NOT THAT I REALLY CARE...
THUNGK
EVERYTHING'S GOING DARK...I'LL JUST... GIVE UP...
MUNCH MUNCH
HEH HEH HEH...
WHAT?! NO! NO, I'M GOING TO LIVE!
YEEAAH!
I HAVE TO BE REUNITED WITH AMY!
SHUPT...
WHAT?!

YOU'RE GOING TO KEEP LIVING?!
SERIOUSLY?!
?
ULPT!
URRGH
KOFF KOFF
TUMP TUMP
YOU SHOCKED ME SO MUCH THAT I GOT GRASS STUCK IN MY THROAT!
GRASS?!
FWUMP
OH FORGET IT. I'LL JUST GIVE UP.
KOFF...
WHAAAAT?!
SHUP
HMM... I SURVIVED...
HE'S STILL EATING GRASS?!

MUNCH MUNCH

I'M A HERBIVORE YO-KAI THAT AVOIDS COMPETITION AND CONFLICT.

I PREFER TO LIVE A LIFE OF UTTER PEACE AND QUIET.

HERBIVORE YO-KAI

HERBIBOY

MEEOOW!

BUT THAT'S SO DULL!

WHAT A PLAIN, BORING ABILITY! GET OUT OF HERE! WHO NEEDS YA?!

WHAT?

THE FISH PLACE
FISH
YOU GO AWAY!
I LIKE IT HERE AND DON'T WANT TO MOVE!
WAIT...YOU'RE ENGAGING IN CONFLICT! WHAT ABOUT YOUR BIG INTRODUCTION?!

THIS PLACE HAS EXCELLENT GRASS! ♪
AHA! YOU WANT THE GRASS FOR YOURSELF!
OF COURSE I DON'T. JUST LEAVE ALREADY...
WHAAAAA

PAWS OF FURY!
VIO-LENCE ISN'T THE ANSWER!
GIVE PEACE A CHANCE!
SAFETY FIRST!
STAY IN SCHOOL!
WHAT?! YOU'RE JUST GOING TO SHOUT SLOGANS AT ME?!

HRRNNGH
THAT WAS SO EASY...
I AVOID FIGHTS BECAUSE OF HOW WEAK I AM...
BUT IF YOU GIVE IT YOUR ALL, YOU'LL NEVER HAVE REGRETS, EVEN IF YOU LOSE!
MAYBE YOU'RE RIGHT. I'LL TRY TO BE MORE LIKE YOU AND GIVE IT MY ALL!
MUNCH MUNCH
CHOMP CHOMP
I HAVE TO KEEP EATING GRASS FOR ENERGY! ♪
THAT'S THE SPIRIT! ♪
OH.
SHIP...
?

URRGH! IT'S STUCK IN MY THROAT!
COUGH COUGH
URRRRGH.
NOT AGAIN!
TUMP TUMP
UNNNH
WHAT?! JUST WHEN YOU WERE GOING TO GIVE IT YOUR ALL!
SHWIP
OH? HE'S COMING BACK!
FISH
THE AFTERLIFE WAS SO FAR AWAY... SO I DECIDED NOT TO BOTHER GOING.
I'LL MAKE AN EFFORT TO TRY AND DO MY BEST.
SWIP
I... GUESS THAT COUNTS AS MOTIVATION?

CHAPTER 121: LISTENING YO-KAI NAANDHI

...
TELL ME WHAT'S TROUBLING YOU.
WELL...I KEEP FIGHTING ALL THESE TRUCKS, BUT I CAN NEVER BEAT THEM.
...

HMM, IS THAT SO?

FISH

END OF THE YEAR / NEW YEAR'S SHOP OPENING SCHEDULE

TELL ME WHAT'S TROUBLING YOU.

FISH

TELL ME WHAT'S

FISH

END OF THE YEAR / NEW YEAR'S SHOP OPENING SCHEDULE

TELL ME WHAT'S

WAIT... THAT'S IT?! YOU JUST LISTEN?!
THAT'S RIGHT. I'M A LISTEN-ING YO-KAI
LISTENING YO-KAII
NAANDHI

YO-KAI ARE SUPPOSED TO **DO SOMETHING** WHEN THEY INSPIRIT SOMEONE!

WE'RE SUPPOSED TO BE LIKE, "OH, IT WAS BECAUSE OF A YO-KAI" WHEN SOMETHING HAPPENS! THAT'S HOW THIS WORKS!

IS THAT SO?

WHAAAAA

ARR-RRGH!

I'D PUNCH YOU IF YOU WEREN'T AN OLD MAN!
...
YEAH, YEAH, I KNOW! YOU'RE JUST GONNA SAY, "IS THAT SO?" AGAIN, RIGHT?

SWAAAPT
HUURGH!
YOU FOOL!
AS LONG AS YOU KEEP RELYING ON VIOLENCE TO SOLVE YOUR PROBLEMS ...
...YOU'LL NEVER ACHIEVE YOUR GOAL!
WHY'S HE SCOLD-ING ME ALL OF A SUDDEN ?!
HEY! HOW CAN YOU TELL ME NOT TO USE VIOLENCE AFTER YOU JUST ATTACKED ME?!

BAAAM
I DIDN'T USE VIOLENCE. I JUST SMACKED YOU WITH A NAAN! ♪
ARE YOU SERIOUS?
LIKE I'M GOING TO FALL FOR THAT!
SWAPT
SWAPT
WHAT?! ARE YOU MOCKING ME?!
THIS IS VIO-LENCE!
SWAPT
SWAPT
NAAN IS A TYPE OF INDIAN BREAD EATEN WITH CURRY.
I WAS HOLDING BACK BECAUSE YOU'RE AN OLD MAN, BUT I'VE HAD ENOUGH OF THIS!
HA HA HA ...

I MAY LOOK OLD, BUT I'M ACTUALLY ONLY 17...
HA HA HA...
WHHAAAAAA
YOU'RE SO YOUNG!
JUST KIDDING! ♪ I'M NOT ACTUALLY. ♪
...
HEY! THIS IS YOUR CHANCE TO SAY IT! TO GO, "IS THAT SO?" WHY AREN'T YOU SAYING IT?!
WHAA?!
THAT'S IT...
...I'M GOING TO CLOBBER YOU!
GRRRR

THOOM
THOOM
THOOM
NNGH
TWITCH
TWITCH
YOU'RE... STRONGER THAN I THOUGHT...
OH NO, HE'S SO OLD...I REALLY OVERDID IT!
IT'S OKAY... DON'T WORRY ABOUT IT...
NNNG
GASP... GASP...
I FEEL AWFUL!
I'M SORRY I WENT TOO FAR.
OVER-DOING IT MEANS YOU LOST YOUR COOL...
...AND IF YOU LOSE YOUR COOL IN BATTLE...
...YOU'LL ALSO LOSE THE FIGHT!
!!!
I SEE! DID YOU... DID YOU LOSE ON PURPOSE JUST TO TEACH ME THAT LESSON?
NO... YOU JUST BEAT ME UP REALLY BAD.
Urgh...
VRROOM
LOOK! A TRUCK! I'LL CHAL-LENGE IT!
YOU HAVE TO STAY CALM!
MEOW!

KA-THUNK!
ARRRRRRGH!
...

YOU JUST DON'T HAVE WHAT IT TAKES.
IS...IS THAT SO...?

CHAPTER 122:
WITCH GIRL YO-KAI
MAGINYAN
I THINK I'VE GATHERED ENOUGH!
THE LEAVES ARE ON THE GROUND... ♪ ...LIGHT IT UP AND GO TO TOWN... ♪ ...I'M GONNA BASK IN THE GLOW... ♪
...AND BAKE THIS SWEET POTATO! ♪
...
WHAAAAAA
I DON'T HAVE ANY MATCHES!
I forgot to bring them!
YOU NEED FIRE? LEAVE IT TO ME! ♪
FOOO
OOO. ♪

FWOOOSH!
FIRE!
GO!
AHHH!
FWOOOSH
ARR-RRRGH! DON'T SHOOT IT AT ME!
OH NO! SORRY!
SOME-TIMES MY AIM IS OFF!
SIZZLE SIZZLE...
...
THEN YOU SHOULDN'T BE THROW-ING FIRE AROUND!
PFFFT
YOU'RE RIGHT! HA HA! ♪
IT'S NOT A LAUGHING MATTER!

MY NAME IS MAGINYAN. ♪
Nice to meet you. ♪
WITCH GIRL YO-KAI
MAGINYAN
YOU'RE A... WITCH?!
LIKE THE MONSTERS THAT CURSE PEOPLE AND GIVE THEM POISONED APPLES?!
THAT'S RIGHT! ♪ I'VE EVEN GOT AN APPLE RIGHT HERE! ♪
WOULD YOU LIKE IT?
FSSH
NO THANK YOU.
I JUST WANT TO BAKE THIS SWEET POTATO...
OKAY, NO PRO-BLEM! ♪
ONE MORE TRY!
FOOOO
PLEASE AIM CARE-FULLY...
IF YOU'RE WORRIED, JUST GET OUT OF THE WAY! ♪
OKAY...
FIRE! GO!

FWOOOOOOSH!

I CAN'T DODGE THAT!

ALL YOU DO IS COMPLAIN!
EVERYONE MAKES MISTAKES, YOU KNOW!
FIRE IS TOO DANGER-OUS TO MAKE MISTAKES WITH!
JUST KNOCK IT OFF!
GRRRRRR! I'LL BURN YOU TO ASHES! EAT FLAME!
FWOOO
HEY... YOU'RE SCARING ME!
FIRE! GO!
FWOOOM
ARRRRRGH!

WHAT?! NO!

FWOOOSH!

THE FIRE'S ATTACKING HER?! SHE'S TERRIBLE AT THIS...

YOU'RE UNBELIEVABLE... WATER! WE NEED WATER!

HOT! HOT!

I KNOW! I'LL PUT IT OUT WITH MAGIC!

BLIZZARD! GO!

FWOOOOOM

OOOO! THAT'S A GREAT IDEA! ♪

WHAAAAT?! WHY DID IT FREEZE YOU?!
KRRRAK
I...WAS GOING TO ASK...THE SAME... THING...
I KNOW! GRAB AHOLD OF ME!
SIZZLE
SIZZLE
FWOO
FWOO
I GET IT! USE THE ICE TO PUT OUT THE FIRE!
AND USE THE FIRE TO MELT THE ICE! A TWO-FOR-ONE DEAL! ♪
GLOMP
FSSSSSSH
EXACTLY! ♪

AIYEEEEEE!
URRGH! WHY COULDN'T YOU BE MORE CAREFUL?!
KRRRKT
HNNGH
HMM... A SPELL THAT PUTS BROKEN THINGS BACK TO-GETHER ...
PLEASE... DON'T TRY TO FIX IT...
THEY FIGURED IT OUT AFTER A FEW DAYS...

CHAPTER 123:
NO-GOOD YO-KAI
NUMMSKULL
WHAAAAAAAT?!
SHOOOOOOOK
I WAS GOING T NATE'S HOUSE BU SOMEHO ENDED U AT THE OCEAN.
WHAAAT?!
SHWAAA
I MUST HAVE BEEN DAY-DREAMING!
I NEED TO BE MORE CARE-FUL.
SH-SHWAAA
HEH HEH HEH ...

WHAAAAAAAT?!
NOW I'M IN THE MIDDLE OF THE FOREST!
SHFF
EEEEEEK!
HOW DO I KEEP GETTING LOST?! WHERE AM I?!
VERY IMPRES-SIVE! I'VE NEVER SEEN SOMEONE BECOME THIS MUCH OF A STUMBLE-BUM!
...
SHFF
SHFF
!!!
OH! THERE YOU ARE!
SWIP
?

MY NAME IS NUMMSKULL !!
PEOPLE I INSPIRIT BECOME HOPELESS STUMBLE-BUMS!
IN OTHER WORDS, THEY BECOME KLUTZES! AWKWARD FOOLS! TOTALLY INEPT!
NO-GOOD YO-KAI
NUMMSKULL
...
OH, YOU'RE OVER THERE.
SWIP
YOU CAN'T EVEN KEEP TRACK OF WHO YOU'RE TALKING TO... YOU'RE THE KLUTZ!
WHAAAAAAT?!
IT'S ONE THING TO CALL MYSELF THAT, BUT I CAN'T STAND OTHER PEOPLE SAYING IT!
BAAAM
APOLOGIZE TO ME
I'M OVER HERE ...
SO ANNOYING.
WHY ARE YOU DOING ALL THIS?!
WHY ...?!
HEH HEH HEH... I DON'T WANT TO BE THE ONLY STUMBLEBUM.
RMBBBLEE
SO ...

...I'M GOING TO DRAG EVERY-ONE DOWN WITH ME!
SPLUB...
ARRRGH! I STEPPED IN POOP!
Filthy animals!
THU NCK
UGGGH!
...
FWUMPT
ARE YOU A KLUTZ OR JUST REALLY UNLUCKY?

SPLUUB...

EWWW... Something smells...

YOU FELL RIGHT BACK INTO THE POOP YOU STEPPED IN!

You just can't win!

THIS IS ALL BECAUSE I INSPIRITED YOU!

YOU MUST BE A BAD LUCK YO-KAI!

SHFF SHFF

SURE. IF THAT'S WHAT YOU THINK, THEN JUST STOP INSPIRITING ME.

LATER.

WAAAAUUGH!

WHAT IS IT THIS TIME?

SHFF

DID YOU STEP IN POOP AGAIN?

OWW...

SOB SOB...

ARE YOU UPSET ABOUT HOW CLUMSY YOU ARE?

NO...

THE POOP IS STINGING MY EYES!
NNG... NNG
WELL... THIS IS A FIRST.

ZZZ...

GRRRRRRR

HE'S NOT EVEN LISTEN-ING!

PAWS OF FURY!

WHAT?! WHY ARE YOU PUNCH-ING ME?!

SPLOOS
AHHH!

KSSSHHHH
GRRR! I'LL TURN YOU INTO A TOTAL, COM-PLETELY IRREDEEM-ABLE KLUTZ!
SOUL-TIMATE MOVE, NUMM-SKULL DEMISE!

NUMMSKULL DEMISE IS NUMMSKULL'S SOULTIMATE MOVE IN WHICH HE SELF-DESTRUCTS, TURNING EVERYONE AROUND HIM INTO A KLUTZ!
YOU'RE GOING TO SELF-DESTRUCT?! ARE YOU NUTS?! STOP IT!

I REFUSE!
WE EE

EAT THIS!

KRA-DOOM

SHWAAAA

THE RIVER IS CARRYING HIM AWAY...

It was all... pointless.

SHWAAA
SHWAAAA
...

HUNH
WHAT A KLUTZ...

NO... I'LL NEVER... NEVER FORGIVE HIM! THAT...
HUH...? WHAT WAS HIS NAME AGAIN...?
SIZZLE SIZZLE...
PLIP
IF EVERYTHING KEEPS GOING WRONG FOR YOU, YOU MIGHT BE INSPIRITED BY NUMMSKULL!

CHAPTER 124:
KICKBACK YO-KAI
ULTERIA

I COM-PLETELY FORGOT TO DO MY HOME-WORK!
ARRRGGH!
IT'S TOO LATE TO DO ANYTHING ABOUT IT. YOU'RE GOING TO GET IN TROUBLE.
HERE, NATE. USE THIS.
MATH
OOO! I CAN COPY IT?! THANKS, BEAR!
NO PROBLEM.
RRMMBLEE

NATE! THIS IS NOT OKAY!
HOMEWORK ISN'T JUST BUSYWORK--IT HELPS YOU LEARN BY REVIEWING WHAT WAS COVERED IN CLASS AND GETTING YOU READY FOR THE NEXT DAY!
COPYING SOMEONE ELSE'S HOMEWORK MIGHT SAVE YOU TIME NOW, BUT IT'S ONLY GOING TO HURT YOU IN THE LONG RUN!
IF YOU REALLY THINK ABOUT IT, COPYING IS JUST A WASTE OF TIME, AS YOU'LL LEARN NEITHER THE MATERIAL IN THE LESSON NOR THE IMPORTANCE OF ACTUALLY DOING YOUR HOMEWORK! **UNDERSTAND?**
WHISPER.
SO YOU GET IT?
WHAAAAAAA
GET OUT OF THE WAY. YOU'RE BLOCKING THE NOTEBOOK.
DING DONG DING
BYE-BYE. ♪
HA HA HA HA
BYE!
WHISPER... I WAS WRONG...
SEE?

AHH... THIS IS REALLY GREAT! ♪
Thanks so much for returning the favor! ♪
URGH...I DIDN'T REALIZE... HE WAS GOING TO ORDER ME AROUND... TO REPAY HIM...
I SHOULD HAVE... DONE MY HOME-WORK...
THAT'S GOOD TO HEAR, NATE!
BUT SINCE IT WAS ME THAT HELPED YOU LEARN THAT LESSON...
...YOU CAN CARRY ME ANOTHER 300 FEET TO THANK ME!
NO WAY!
WHAT?!
WHAAAAT?!
GRRRRRR
I TAUGHT YOU THE IMPORTANCE OF DOING YOUR HOMEWORK AND YOU'RE NOT EVEN GOING TO THANK ME?!
WHY ARE YOU BEING SO CONDE-SCEND-ING?!
FWAAASH
COULD IT BE...

MAYBE IT'S A... CAULDRON-CENDING YO-KAI OR SOME-THING?!
WELL, ACTUALLY...
THERE'S NO SUCH YO-KAI, NATE...
HMM... ALL I SEE...
...IS THIS MYSTERI-OUS YO-KAI OVER HERE!
AHHHH
SO THERE IS A YO-KAI AFTER ALL! WHY DIDN'T YOU SAY SO?!
FSH...
HA HA. ♪

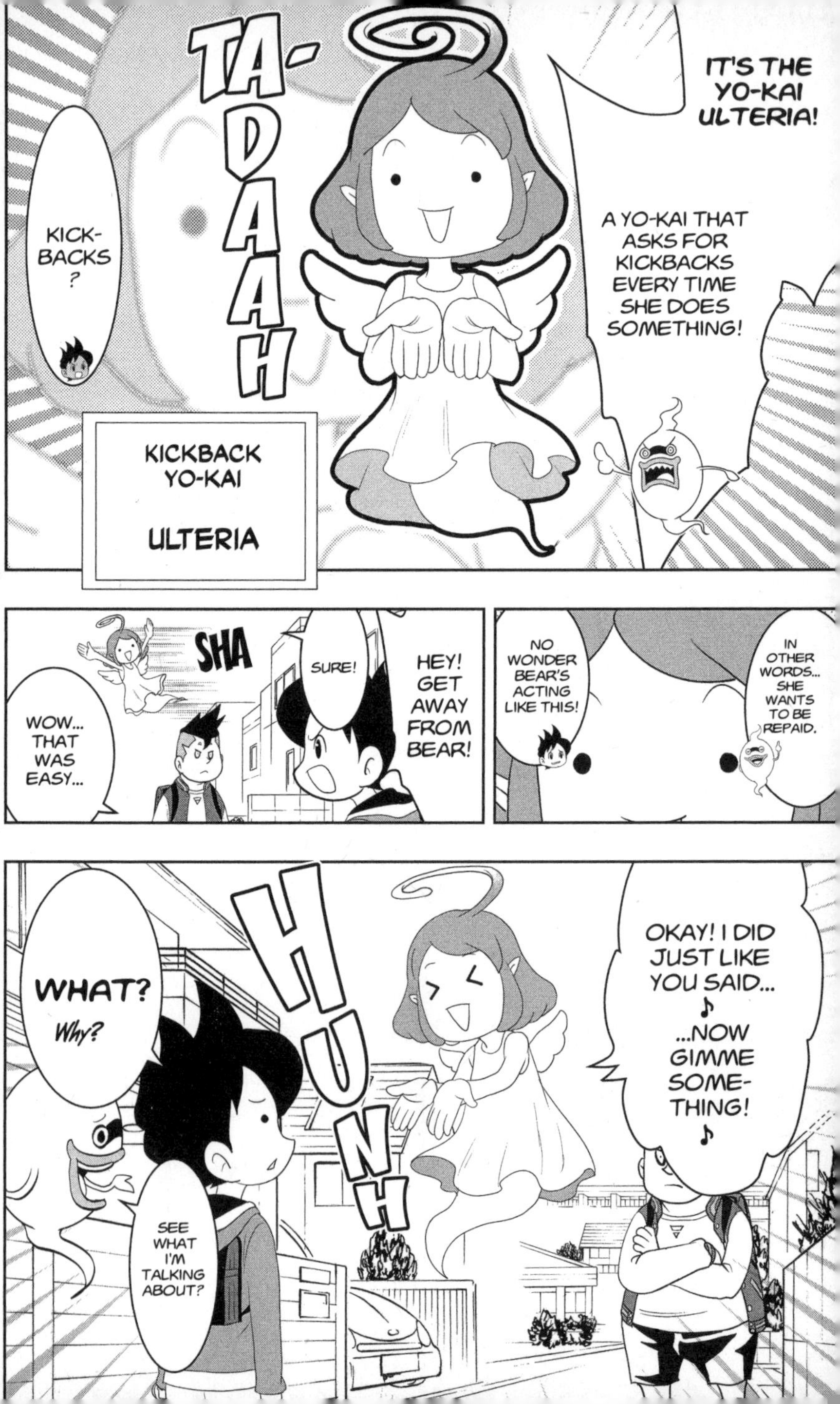

TA-DAAAH

IT'S THE YO-KAI ULTERIA!

A YO-KAI THAT ASKS FOR KICKBACKS EVERY TIME SHE DOES SOMETHING!

KICK-BACKS?

KICKBACK YO-KAI

ULTERIA

IN OTHER WORDS... SHE WANTS TO BE REPAID.

NO WONDER BEAR'S ACTING LIKE THIS!

HEY! GET AWAY FROM BEAR!

SURE!

SHA

WOW... THAT WAS EASY...

OKAY! I DID JUST LIKE YOU SAID... ♪ ...NOW GIMME SOME-THING! ♪

HUNH

WHAT? *Why?*

SEE WHAT I'M TALKING ABOUT?

NATE... AREN'T YOU GOING TO HELP BEAR?
IT SERVES HIM RIGHT FOR ORDERING ME AROUND.
OKAY...KEEP INSPIRITING HIM THEN.
IT'S JUST GOING TO RUIN BEAR'S REPUTATION. IT'S NOT MY PROBLEM.
YOU MONSTER! HOW COULD YOU?!
YOU'RE ABSOLUTELY TERRIBLE! YOU'RE JUST GOING TO USE AND ABANDON ME LIKE THIS?!

OH NOOOO! I WAS TALKING TO A YO-KAI IN FRONT OF SOMEONE WHO CAN'T SEE THEM! AND EVEN WORSE...I WAS TALKING BAD ABOUT HIM!
AGGGGH!
...
WHAT DO YOU MEAN? ARE YOU JUST BABBLING TO YOURSELF OR WHAT?

HMMMM
I GET IT NOW! NATE...
UHM...
A... YO-KAI...?
YOU BRING THEM UP KINDA FRE-QUENTLY...

...YOU MUST LIVE IN SOME KINDA FANTASY WORLD. THAT'S WHY YOU FORGOT YOUR HOMEWORK.

REIN IT IN, MAN.

Later.

I'M GLAD HE'S SLOW TO CATCH ON...

...
WHY AREN'T YOU FOLLOWING HIM?
...

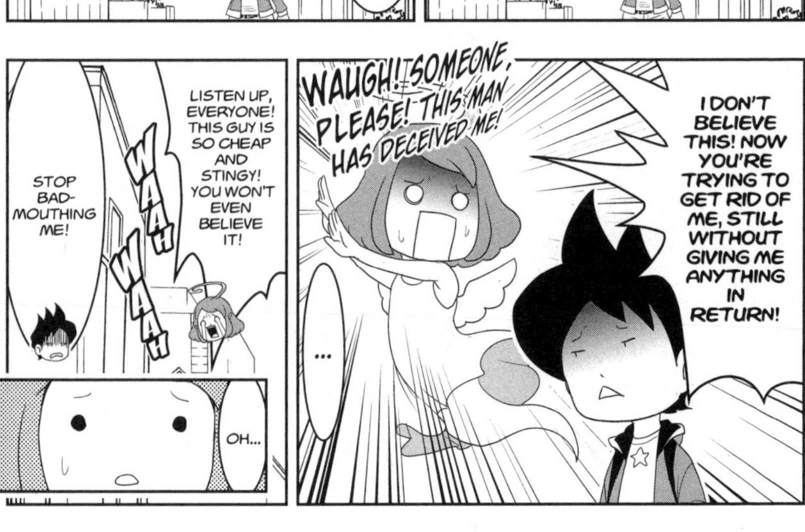

I DON'T BELIEVE THIS! NOW YOU'RE TRYING TO GET RID OF ME, STILL WITHOUT GIVING ME ANYTHING IN RETURN!
WAUGH! SOMEONE, PLEASE! THIS MAN HAS DECEIVED ME!
...
LISTEN UP, EVERYONE! THIS GUY IS SO CHEAP AND STINGY! YOU WON'T EVEN BELIEVE IT!
WAAH WAAH
STOP BAD-MOUTHING ME!
OH...

AHHHH
...SO YOU ARE GOING TO GIVE ME SOMETHING THEN! ♪
THIS ISN'T JUST ASKING FOR KICKBACKS... YOU'RE BLACK-MAILING ME!
I'VE HAD ENOUGH! I'M GOING TO TEACH YOU A LESSON!
YO-KAI MEDAL, DO YOUR THING!
KRRRKT
CALLING ...
... LAST NYAN-MURAI!
VRRRrRN
I SEE! NYANMURAI ACTS SELF-LESSLY AND RESPECT-FULLY! YOU'RE GOING TO TEACH HER HOW TO DO THE SAME!

KA-THNK

WHAT HAPPENED?

SQUEEEEE
WHY IS IT JUST YOUR HEAD?!
URRGH ...!
LET GO! LET ME GO!
HEY! STOP-PIT!
WAIT...IS THERE SOME-ONE ELSE THERE?!
MEEEOOW!
GRRRP
HE'S GETTING SUCKED BACK IN! THIS HAS NEVER HAPPENED BEFORE!
...
HE'S COMING BACK OUT!

MEEEOOOW!
TOMNYAN?!
YEAH, I KNOW! YOU NEVER CALL ME! SO I KEPT AN EYE ON JIBANYAN SINCE YOU CALL HIM ALL THE TIME...
...I WAS JUST WAITING FOR MY OPPOR-TUNITY!
WHAT?! I DIDN'T CALL FOR YOU!
EVER SINCE I DEBUTED, I HAVEN'T HAD MUCH TO DO IN THE MANGA. AND ON TOP OF THAT...

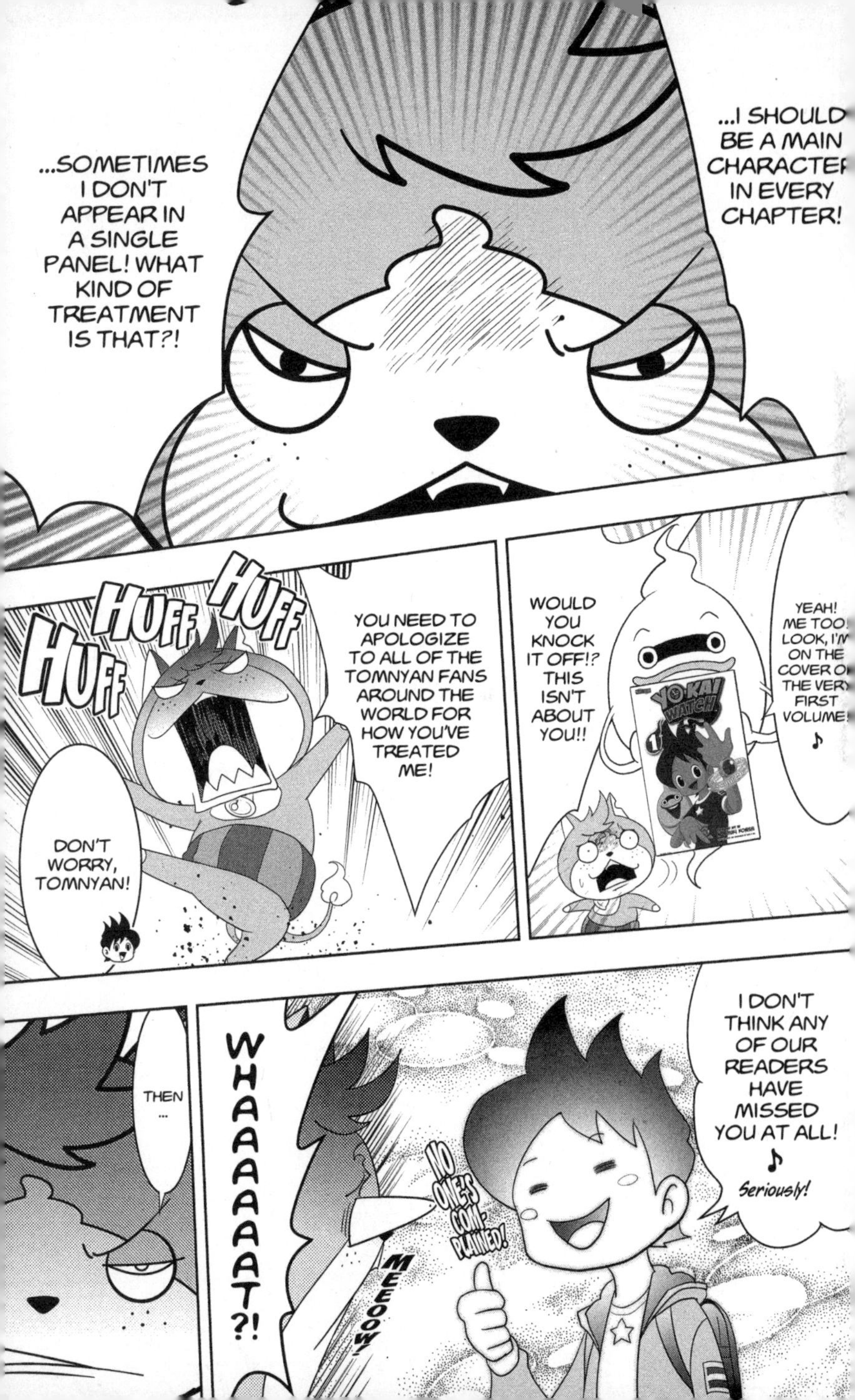

...I SHOULD BE A MAIN CHARACTER IN EVERY CHAPTER!
...SOMETIMES I DON'T APPEAR IN A SINGLE PANEL! WHAT KIND OF TREATMENT IS THAT?!
YEAH! ME TOO! LOOK, I'M ON THE COVER OF THE VERY FIRST VOLUME! ♪
YO-KAI WATCH
WOULD YOU KNOCK IT OFF!? THIS ISN'T ABOUT YOU!!
YOU NEED TO APOLOGIZE TO ALL OF THE TOMNYAN FANS AROUND THE WORLD FOR HOW YOU'VE TREATED ME!
HUFF HUFF HUFF
DON'T WORRY, TOMNYAN!
I DON'T THINK ANY OF OUR READERS HAVE MISSED YOU AT ALL! ♪
Seriously!
NO ONE'S COM-PLAINED!
WHAAAAAAAAAT?!
MEEEOOW!
THEN ...

AWWWWW
...JUST FORGET ABOUT IT.
YOU'RE SULKING ...?
AND JIBANYAN ISN'T COMING OUT...?
HMPH
I CON-VINCED HIM TO GIVE ME THE LEADING ROLE BEFORE I CAME OUT...
YOU MEAN... BY FORCE ?!
GULP...
NO WAY. HE WAS THRILLED FOR A DAY OFF!
YEEAAH!
OH REALLY ...
BUT I DON'T EVEN CARE WHAT HAPPENS IN THIS MANGA ANYMORE.
HMPH
NOW NOW ...
LEAVE IT TO ME! ♪ I'LL MAKE THIS MANGA EXCITING AGAIN! ♪
WHAT?

JUST GIMME SOMETHING IN RETURN!
B-BAAM
THAT'S ENOUGH! JUST GET OUT OF HERE!
OKAY I'LL LEAVE ...
...IF YOU GIMME SOME-THING.
AGGGH, SHE'S SO ANNOY-ING!
TOMNYAN! COULD YOU CHASE HER AWAY?!
!
PLEASE!
AHA! FINALLY! AN OPPORTUNIT FOR ME TO SHINE!
VSH
I'LL BECOME THE MAIN CHARACTER BY DRIVING HER AWAY IN AN IMPRESSIVE FASHION!
!!!
WOOO
CENTI ...
OSH

...CUFFS!

CHOOM CHOOM CHOOM CHOOM CHOOM

EEEEEK!!!

I'LL GIVE YOU SOME-THING IF YOU HELP ME!

SHUPT

WHAT?

WHAAAAAT?!

OOOF! AGGGH! URGH!
THUD
THUD
WHISPEEEEER!

THANK YOU FOR SAVING ME...
Are you okay?
TWITCH TWITCH...
I...I NEVER MEANT... TO HELP YOU...
OH...THEN I GUESS I DON'T HAVE TO THANK YOU! ♪
AN APOLOGY... WOULD BE NICE THOUGH...

LET'S TRY THIS AGAIN!
VOOSH
!!!
GRRRR

SHUPT
STOP IT!
YOU'RE HURTING HIM!
WHAT?! YOU'RE USING HIM AS A SHIELD AGAIN?!
URRRGGH
TWITCH TWITCH...
TOMNYAN! I NEED YOU TO GET RID OF HER WITH-OUT USING FORCE!
!!!
SHA
WHAT?! THAT HUMAN'S PROTECT-ING ME?!
IT'S SUP-POSE TO BE ME, ISN'T IT?
I CAN'T SLOW DOWN!
CHOM CHOM
CHOM CHOM
AGGGGH!

!!!
SHOOF
ARRRRRRRRGH!
CHOOM CHOOM CHOOM CHOOM CHOOM CHOOM
ARE... ARE YOU OKAY...?
I...THINK SO... THANKS...
I REPAID YOU... BECAUSE ...
...YOU PROTECTED ME FIRST! ♪
WHAT?

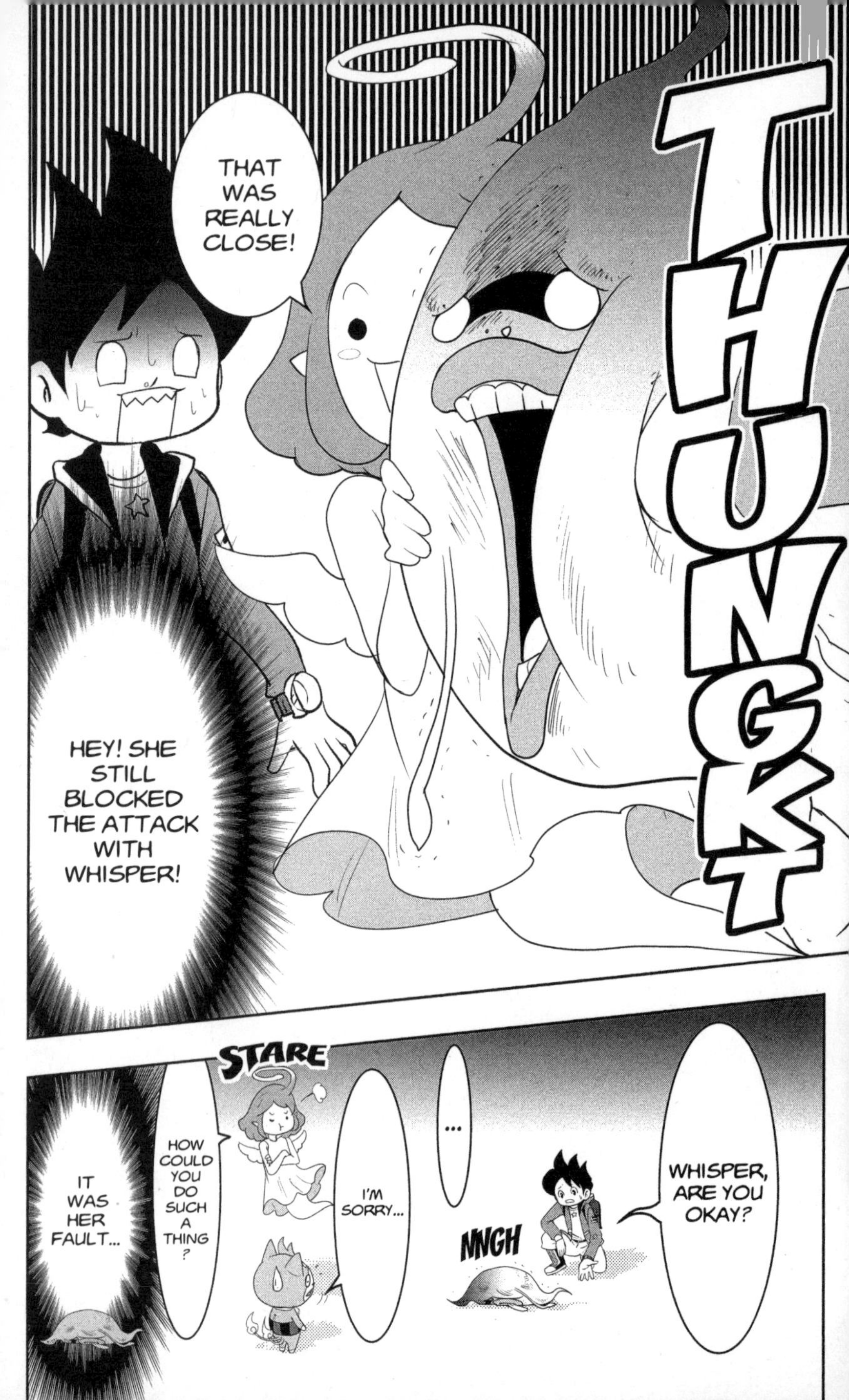
THUNGK
THAT WAS REALLY CLOSE!
HEY! SHE STILL BLOCKED THE ATTACK WITH WHISPER!
WHISPER, ARE YOU OKAY?
NNGH
...
I'M SORRY...
STARE
HOW COULD YOU DO SUCH A THING?
IT WAS HER FAULT...

YOU DON'T ONLY ASK FOR KICKBACKS, DO YOU? YOU ALSO REPAY PEOPLE!
OF COURSE!
BUT...IT WAS ME... THAT HELPED YOU...!
HELPING OTHERS IS ONLY NATURAL...
...AND SO IS PAYING THEM BACK WHEN THEY HELP YOU! ♪
I THOUGHT SHE ONLY EVER ASKED FOR THINGS AND NEVER HELPED OUT...
HAHAHA
ANYWAY, SINCE I JUST HELPED YOU...
...GIMME SOME-THING IN RETURN!
SHE REALLY STICKS TO HER PLANS...
WELL... WHAT DO YOU WANT?

FOR YOU TO BE MY FRIEND! ♪

WHAT?

I FIGURE EVERY TIME YOU SUMMON ME...

...YOU'LL END UP GIVING ME SOMETHING! ♪

HEE HEE HEE.

THAT'S SO SELF-SERVING!

NO IT'S NOT!

...

I'VE BEFRIENDED A LOT OF YO-KAI...
...AND I ALWAYS THINK ABOUT ASKING THEM FOR HELP LATER!
BUT ASKING PEOPLE FOR KICKBACKS ALL THE TIME...

FRIENDS SHOULD ALWAYS THANK EACH OTHER PROPERLY.
GIVE AND TAKE IS NATURAL IN A FRIENDSHIP! ♪ RIGHT?
...
BAAM
WHY ARE YOU OKAY WITH THIS?! FRIENDS SHOULDN'T USE EACH OTHER AS SHIELDS!!!
HA HA. ♪ NICE TO MEET YOU!
YOU TOO! ♪
WHY AREN'T YOU LISTEN-ING TO ME?!
ARRRRGH!

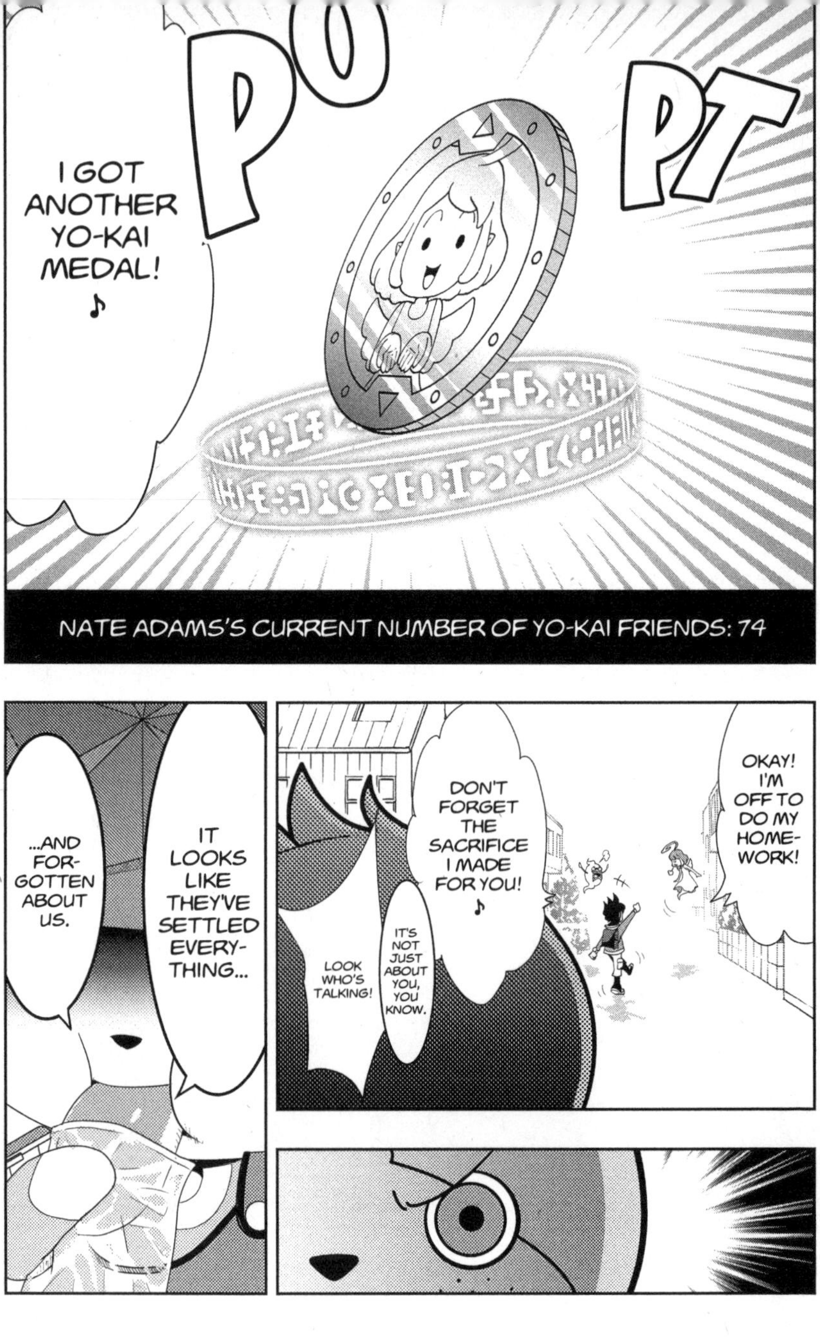

PO PT

I GOT ANOTHER YO-KAI MEDAL! ♪

NATE ADAMS'S CURRENT NUMBER OF YO-KAI FRIENDS: 74

OKAY! I'M OFF TO DO MY HOME-WORK!

DON'T FORGET THE SACRIFICE I MADE FOR YOU! ♪

IT'S NOT JUST ABOUT YOU, YOU KNOW.

LOOK WHO'S TALKING!

IT LOOKS LIKE THEY'VE SETTLED EVERY-THING...

...AND FOR-GOTTEN ABOUT US.

I THINK IT'S ABOUT TIME...
...THAT WE HAD A TALK.
BA
AM
I...

GHOULFATHER ARC BEGINNING IN THE NEXT VOLUME!!

Welcome to the world of Little Battlers eXperience! In the near future, a boy named Van Yamano owns Achilles, a miniaturized robot that battles on command! But Achilles is no ordinary LBX. Hidden inside him is secret data that Van must keep out of the hands of evil at all costs!

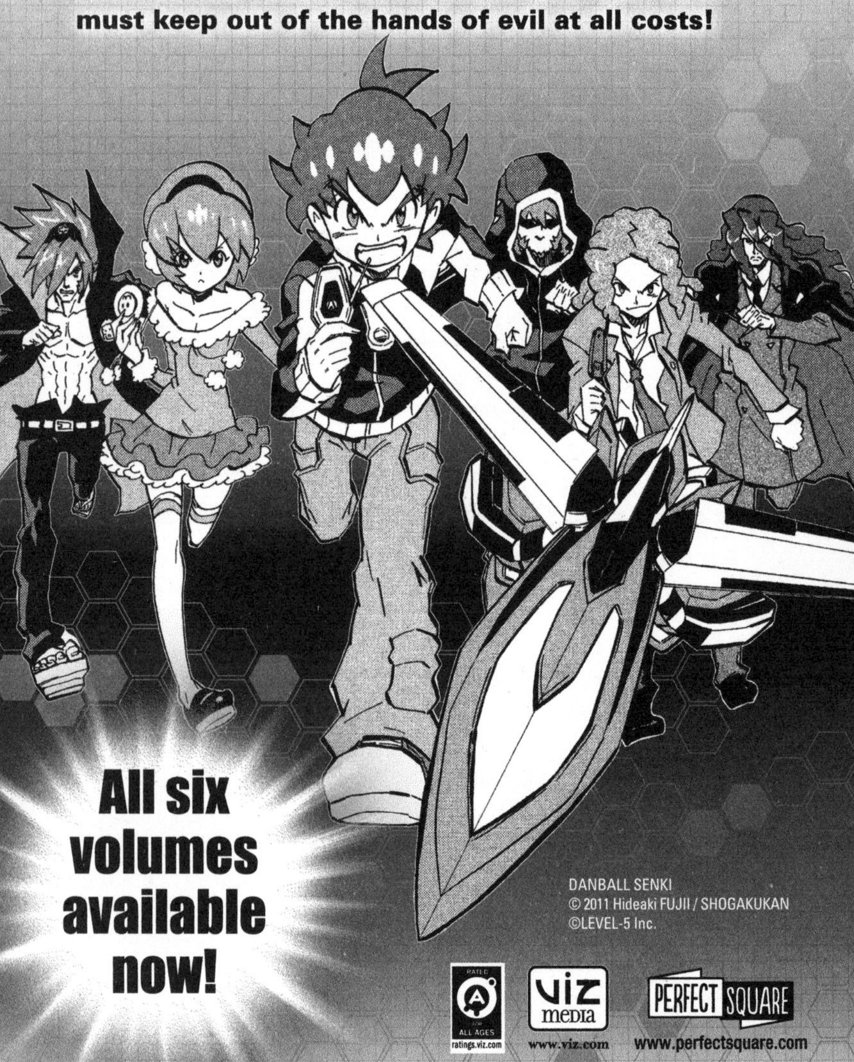

All six volumes available now!

Story and Art by
HIDEAKI FUJII

APPEARANCE

AH!
I HAVEN'T BEEN APPEARING IN THE MANGA RECENTLY ...
COULD IT BE ...?!

MAYBE THE AUTHOR HAS GOTTEN BORED OF ME?!
SHOOCK
HA HA HA. ♪ THAT'S POSSIBLE. ♪
HUMPH.

LOOK WHO'S TALKING! YOU'VE HAD EVEN LESS APPEAR-ANCES THAN ME!!
SHOCK
HUUH ?!
PFFFT. RIGHT. ♪
HUMPH.

...
E-EH, TH-THAT'S OKAY.
UH-HUH...
VEEEEN
DON'T GIVE ME THAT LOOK OF PITY!

TOM-NYAN PLAYS A MAJOR ROLE IN VOLUME 13.

AUTHOR BIO

A kid I signed an autograph for during my *Go-Go-Go Saiyuki* days is my new assistant. I'm not musing about how quickly time moves though. I'm just saying… All nine volumes of *Go-Go-Go Saiyuki* are available now in Japan! You can also get them digitally!
—Noriyuki Konishi

Noriyuki Konishi hails from Shimabara City in Nagasaki Prefecture, Japan. He debuted with the one-shot *E-CUFF* in *Monthly Shonen Jump Original* in 1997. He is known in Japan for writing manga adaptations of *AM Driver* and *Mushiking: King of the Beetles*, along with *Saiyuki Hiro Go-Kū Den!*, *Chōhenshin Gag Gaiden!! Card Warrior Kamen Riders*, *Go-Go-Go Saiyuki: Shin Gokūden* and more. Konishi was the recipient of the 38th Kodansha manga award in 2014 and the 60th Shogakukan manga award in 2015.

THIS IS THE END OF THIS GRAPHIC NOVEL!

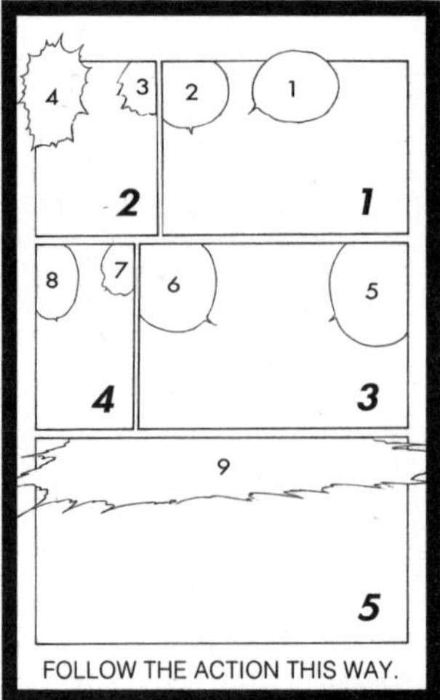

To properly enjoy this graphic novel, please turn it around and begin reading from right to left.